LUCID SCREAMS

Red Lagoe

Lucid Screams

Previously published stories by Red include:

The Haunting Murder: published by *Z Publishing House*, 2018
Luna's Lure: published by *Owl Hollow Press*, 2018
Best Seat in the House: published by *Trembling with Fear,* 2018
Abandoned Souls: Originally published as *Missing Souls* by Z-Publishing
House ©2018 Red Lagoe
Malignant Roots: published by *Crystal Lake Publishing,* 2019
Helping Hands Retreat: published by *Toasted Cheese Literary Journal,* 2017
Odor Mortis: published by *Crystal Lake Publishing,* 2019
Memory Lane: published by *Crystal Lake Publishing,* 2019

ISBN (paperback): #978-0-9988531-2-3
ISBN (e-book): #978-0-9988531-3-0

La
red
LaRed Books

Table of Contents

From the deepest chambers of my black heart, many thanks to:

My critique group friends at Tidewater Writers who have picked apart my first drafts over the past few years—especially my regular victims: Tony, Kate, Melina, Rick, Marilyn, and Amber;

Hampton Roads Writers, who offer free and affordable workshops and professional critiques;

Crystal Lake Publishing for the fantastic career mentorship program—career mentor Joe Mynhardt, and editing mentors, Kenneth W. Cain and Monique Snyman;

Katie and Sandy, my proofreading goddesses;

My number one fan and always the last eyes on my stories, Donna McCracken;

And to Jason, who never doubts my capabilities.

Introduction

STORIES PULL US INTO a dream world where we can escape our problems. Horror, however, does not take us away to spectacular, feel-good lands. It drags us into the darkest depths of our imaginations.

Horror—even when told in fantastic stories of sci-fi or dark comedy—can force us to face our fears, our tragedies, our inner demons. We must stare those beasts in the eye with each turn of the page, and in doing so, we might discover reflections of our inner selves. Shameful slivers of our humanity buried deep beneath our more presentable exteriors. Shocking, formidable splinters that deserve to stay buried. But, more than likely, we'll find strength in ourselves where we didn't know it existed.

When horrors of the real world find me, I can close my eyes and pretend it's all a dream. But in doing so, I am silenced, shriveled in the charred black caverns of despair. Instead, I choose to open my eyes. Lucid and screaming into the face of fear, I challenge the abysmal void, even if I have to burn my own heart to shed a flicker of light.

In the utter darkness, we can always create light.

Fear not, these stories are not *all* downers, full of dread and hopelessness. A few of them are fun supernatural tales of ghosts, aliens, pizza, and even a penis. Yeah, you read that right.

Kick back, open your heart and mind to the genre, and learn a little about yourself. At the very least, you'll learn I may not be right in the head.

-Red Lagoe

WARNING

If you don't like trigger warnings, turn the page now, and don't read the following paragraph:

Some of the following stories may contain content deserving of trigger warnings. To be respectful of those who have experienced the trauma of losing a child, a list of stories with warnings is available at the back of the book on page 210.

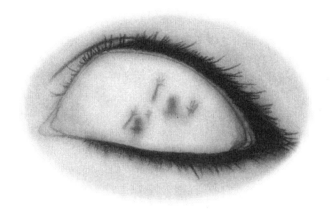

LUCID SCREAMING

THE WALLS ARE BLACK now that the kids are gone. Funny thing is, I don't remember painting them.

Sunrise squeezes through the blinds and orange light streaks the breakfast table. Lily and Ben stare at their dry bowls of cereal. There's no milk. I forgot they were coming to be honest. How am I supposed to remember when it's my weekend or their dad's?

"She didn't get groceries." Lily's words sizzle in the air. She's always putting me down for not being a good enough mom.

"That's okay, Mommy." Naïve unconditional love adorns little Ben's smile.

Lily rolls her eyes—black eyeliner smudged into burn-marks around them.

I point to the mess on her face. "That looks trashy."

"Like you should talk."

Orange sunlight from the kitchen window spreads onto my hands, lighting the peaks of my bulging veins. Crinkled, bruised skin takes the appearance of some alien terrain. Looks like I shot up. Back then, when the veins in my arms were blown, I'd go for the ones in my hands, but I haven't done that in a long time.

I leave the sunlit kitchen and sink into the living room couch. My dark walls provide relief from the heat seeping through the windows. Even though it's morning, the clock on the old VCR still blinks 12:00 like the thing froze in time when Joe and the kids left. He used to fix that stuff, but now he's got some sweet little thing downtown, and all the home repairs are my responsibility. It took all my strength and sanity to fight for the right to see my own kids every other weekend—no wonder the house is falling apart.

"Mommy, look!" Ben says.

"What?" My voice hits barren walls. Walls that used to hold memories of Joe and the kids, but I can't find the time to hang everything back up again. Not really sure where everything is, come to think of it.

"Come see what I built with my Legos." Ben approaches the couch.

I turn to face him, but he isn't there. "Ben?" The house echoes his name in my stolen voice. I push myself up from the couch and scan the room. "Ben?"

Lily, standing in the kitchen doorway, silhouetted in a column of sunlight, crosses her arms. "What are you looking for, Elaine?"

"Call me Mom."

"You lost the right to that title." Her words burn my heart.

"Where's Ben? He just asked me to look at his Legos."

"God, Elaine. That was forever ago."

"That was just now."

Lily gives me a once-over from head to foot. "You're using again, aren't you?"

"No. I gave that up. You know that."

She scuffs at some crud on the floor with the toe of her boot. "You sure about that?"

And for a moment, I'm not certain anymore. Fresh bruises indicate I may have stuck myself recently, but it all seems so foggy. A haze of fragmented memories wisp away with Lily's next question.

"Do you know where your kid is?" she asks. "Do you even know what time it is?"

"Watch it, young lady."

"Or what? What could be worse than right now?"

"Damn you, Lily."

"No. Damn you!" The morning light reflects off her eyes, full of rage and cutting through me.

I turn away from her contempt and continue my search for Ben.

Lily follows with her judgement in tow. "This place looks like shit."

"Lily!" I whip around to give her a piece of my mind, but instead I ask, "Can you help me find your brother?"

Out the foyer window, the rising sun has disappeared, turning the landscape beyond the front porch into a colorless void.

"What's going on?" I back away from the door as nightfall darkens the house in an impossible time shift. "Ben?!" With each shout of his name, my pulse intensifies.

Lily shakes her head. "Losing track of time, Elaine? Maybe if you could stay clean when your kids are visiting. Why do you even bother having us over?"

"Why do *you* even come?" I say. "You're eighteen."

She snarls. "I can't leave you alone with him in case…" She scuffs at the crud on the floor again. Blackened crust peels back from warped linoleum. Lily nods her head toward the hallway. "…in case you forget *you're* responsible for taking care of him."

I push past her and head down the hallway toward Ben's room.

"I wouldn't go in there if I were you." Lily's irises are feathered with a strange orange light. I pause, heeding her warning as her intensity sears my soul.

Within the hall's blackness, I reach for the knob to Ben's door. The landscape of my hand hasn't changed. Orange-topped mountainous veins—as if sunlight was still dancing across them, yet there was no light in the hallway.

I pull my hand from the knob to shake away the illusion.

My daughter's eyes swirl with flames.

"What's happening?" I ask.

A tear trickles down her cheek reflecting a blinding yellow light.

The door to Ben's room opens, but the light switch on his wall doesn't work. The room reeks of burnt plastic. A scant amount of street light seeps in his bedroom window, revealing a blackened tower of blocks as tall as Ben. Behind his bed, in the corner of the room, a shadowy space draws me toward it.

"Ben?" I whisper and turn to Lily, but she is no longer with me. With trepidation, I close in on the charred corner. A small pile of something is bundled within the darkness. I kneel down to investigate and a tiny figure takes shape. A small burned body, curled into the corner.

Heart seizing, body temperature rising, I back out of Ben's room. Sweat drips down my neck and my clothes cling to my body.

"Lily!" I stumble into the hallway.

As I approach her bedroom door, my pulse pounds between my ears. Heat radiates through the wood, and though it is hot to the touch, the door opens without burning my hand.

A pile of books and a laptop sit on the floor in the middle of the room. Like the blocks, they are crusted in a coat of black char. Once-green walls are now glazed with a coal-colored film. Streetlamps from outside highlight a lumpy mass in her twin-sized bed. My pulse goes thick and murky, slows beyond my ability to feel it as I approach her frail remains.

A guttural screech leaves my body. An unrecognizable voice howling from within, mourning, admonishing, cursing.

Stick marks in my hands bleed and drip to the floor.

Fire creeps along the ceiling, filling the room and lighting the bulges in my bleeding veins.

I burst from Lily's room, blood flowing from my hands. Escaping the flames, praying for this to be nothing more than a hallucination—or better yet, a nightmare—I make it to the front door.

Morning sunlight pours inside again, stealing away the darkness.

On the doorstep, Joe holds a bouquet of roses in his arms and he falls to his knees weeping. I try to open the door, but it won't budge, and despite the violent shaking of the knob and thrusting my body weight against the flimsy door, I can't seem to get his attention.

"Joe!" I bang on the window, but he doesn't respond.

He sobs, crumpled on his hands and knees. Then he lays the bouquet on the floorboards out front, stands, and wipes away his tears. On the street, a woman waits for him beside his car—his sweet little thing.

"See you next time, Mommy," Ben says, appearing behind me, untouched by the fire.

I collapse to my knees to hold him, but he vanishes before I can wrap my arms around him. The emptiness within my outstretched arms seeps into my soul and fills me with sickness and aching—worse than the most painful withdrawal.

Lily stands beside me, facing the window.

"Lily?" Her name swims within the void behind my sternum. "What's happening?"

She tilts her head with a sympathetic shrug. "This is *your* weekend. Not ours."

I edge toward her, hopeful to embrace my beloved daughter for the first time in ages, but she shakes her head with disappointment and disappears before I can get close enough.

The floor rushes up on me. Fire creeps into the living room, painting the walls black as it spreads.

"Joe!"

He walks away unresponsive. In the back seat of his car, my children sit bathed in the morning sunlight.

As they pull away, the house fills with smoke, and I crawl toward my bedroom for my cellphone to call for help.

A memory takes hold of my consciousness…

I was in my bedroom, searching for a good enough vein, but I had blown them all. That alone was a sign I shouldn't have been trying to shoot up that night.

A banging on my door sent me scrambling to hide my syringe.

"Mommy! Come see what I built!"

"Not now, Ben." I knew I should stay clean since it was my weekend with the kids.

Lily's voice joined Ben's outside the door. "Come on Ben. I'll tuck you in before I start studying."

I released my held breath and hesitated for a moment, debating whether to suffer through the night of withdrawal, or take the last little bit. The kids' footsteps faded down the hallway, and I injected the last of my stash into my bloodstream.

Smoke fills my lungs. Crawling my way down the hallway through the thick cloud, I cough, conjuring a continuation of the memory...

As I lay in a heroin-induced fog, a cigarette that dangled from my lips fell to the bed. It burned a small hole into the comforter. The blackness spread across the fabric, the smoke gagged me, and I allowed it to as I melted into the comfort of my bed.

The memory lifts again as I crawl out of the fire and into my bedroom.

Inside has been untouched by flames. It's peaceful, but the smell of death lingers. I sit on the edge of my bed and forget for a moment why I entered, or what I was doing.

A burned body lays beside me—a charred frame with a melted rubber tourniquet around her arm. I lie beside myself as the cigarette from my memory burns a hole into the mattress inches away. The fire ignites, but I remain in my bed.

Facing the ceiling, I become one with the scorched body. Paralyzed. Engulfed in the raging flames. There is no way to escape this bed, or this house, or my mistakes.

Bleeding veins pop and boil. Flesh blisters in the searing heat, and skin—once warm and welcoming for my newborn babies—peels and melts away from muscle and bone. Agonizing cries are choked by the billowing black smoke.

However, the sounds from the next room burn more than this fire. Lily, as she awakens to the flames, cries out for help. Then Ben's sweet little voice joins in. Their shrieks of pain and desperation are a red hot spear, pulled from burning embers and thrust through my heart.

Unrelenting screams torture me, and I burn. While listening to the terrified calls for help from my children, I burn. With no mother to comfort them, to save them, they suffer, and I burn, again and again.

I wake up and shuffle through the living room in a haze. Orange sunrise filters in the kitchen window as the clock on the VCR blinks 12:00.

The walls are black now that the kids are gone. Funny thing is, I don't remember painting them.

THE HAUNTING MURDER

FROM THE YARD, Hank heard them coming—a distant, electrical hum on the horizon. As the smoky, black mass in the sky encroached, the screeching static pierced his ears. A myriad of crows undulated above as they closed in, then roosted on the towering rock walls surrounding him. Interlaced with the voices of the crows, a woman's gasp screeched. A familiar, breathy shriek. Hank squeezed his temples to make the hallucination of her voice cease, but it persisted.

Each fall for as long as Hank could remember, sixty thousand crows swarmed the city of Auburn during their migration, isolating their murder to the area around the maximum security prison. And each year, Hank avoided them because of what happened decades ago while twelve year old Hank sat on his bike outside the walls.

The silhouettes of the naked trees against the setting sun were adorned with false leaves—black, flapping wings took the place of the fallen foliage. Through those snaking black branches, he hurled rocks. One after the other, until his stone finally smacked into a crow. Gravity yanked its body from the branch, and the bird hit the sidewalk with a meaty thud.

Hank ran to the fallen bird as it twitched and gyrated, unable to lift itself from the cold cement. Black beaded eyes reflected a glimmer of the orange sky and the image of Hank's sardonic glare. He stumbled back, shaken by his own reflection. As the fallen crow's tremors pulsed to a stop, and before it took its last breath, Hank rode away. The birds overhead screamed and furiously shifted positions on their branches as he pedaled down the street, leaving it to die alone on the winter-parched sidewalk.

He never intended to return to those walls because of those angry and sorrowful cries, but justice summoned him back for his final years.

While he paced the prison yard, sixty thousand squawking screams judged the man inside, who had more than the blood of an old bird on his hands now. Hank blocked out his senses with his hands over his ears and his eyes shut, but feathers thrashed near his face, demanding his attention. A single swooping crow landed beside him.

Its black and gray eyes mirrored the overcast sky, seeking answers, but Hank had none. He searched for his own reflection, as if to see the same child's visage from years ago staring back at him, but it was not there. Instead, a soulless void filled the crow's eye, until it appeared to him—not Hank, but someone else—as a projected image deep inside the tiny, cloud-reflected

21

orb. A closer investigation revealed the gaunt and blood-soaked woman in the green dress. Hank staggered backward as the crow took flight to the top of the wall, cawing in that ghostly woman's voice.

The sound permeated the walls day after day. Batting of wings stirred an uneasy feeling in his gut. Her shrill gasp escaped through the crows' calls, conjuring memories of his victim in the green dress, and the fallen crow from his childhood. The birds' waste splattered onto the cement and painted the prison yard, leaving the taste of culpability on the rim of Hank's state-issued cup. They loomed for months, intimidating, tormenting, haunting. Time went by since they migrated on, but they lingered with him still—absorbed into his subconscious—shrieking obscenities and stirring him from his nightmares.

Each year the murder returned, and each year, it became harder to identify whether the crows were real, or dark apparitions of his fate. His mind edged toward insanity as the relentless calls for justice rang a death knell in his ears.

While Hank was escorted to the chair, the song of the crows loomed in his psyche. The murder perched upon the prison walls while the murderer was strapped to the seat. The woman's scream and the screech of the crows entangled in his mind as the electricity coursed through his body. Shackled to the cold, hard surface, he writhed and twitched as he took one last cacophonous breath, and the crows finally settled into silence.

LUNA'S LURE

OCHER-COLORED LIGHT absorbed into the floorboards of the front porch, bringing a warmth to David's broken home, but not to his weary state. Something was off—in the colors of the sinking sun, in the taste of his cold beer. The orange-yellow light of day faded into a cool gray, bringing with it a warning. A pressure in his chest.

"Full moon tonight." His neighbor Jeff pulled a sip from a chilled amber bottle. "Feels wrong being off duty."

David stood up to break away from the threat within him—that admonishing voice inside whispering to him to get out. To run.

"Where's your boy," Jeff asked.

"Upstairs." David leaned against the porch railing, unable to shake the apprehension. After all, it was the same feeling he had right before finding out his wife was screwing some other guy.

Jeff nodded with what David assumed was judgment and disappointment. Or maybe he had a lot on his mind. Four disappearances, once a month on the full moon, had all of upstate New York on edge. Being Jeff's only confidante made David privy to information police wouldn't even give to the reporters. The first man's disappearance in Ontario County didn't make big news until they found traces of blood and bone fragments behind his work shed. Then came missing cases in Seneca, Cayuga, and Tompkins Counties. Three men, one woman, all had wandered outside around sunset. The only remnants were pools of blood or bits of hair and bone—the rest of their bodies remained missing. Poor bastards. Jeff had said the police in those counties couldn't seem to make any connections between the murders, other than they had all disappeared on a full moon. Then the FBI got involved and took the case from local authorities, leaving Jeff off-duty and sipping a beer with David on a Friday night.

"Still no clues on a suspect?" David asked.

"No clues," Jeff said. "The last woman—there was so much blood. I got to see the photos. Assholes around town making werewolf jokes. They wouldn't be laughing if they saw those photos." He shuddered and set down his beer. "Really feels wrong not working tonight. If this guy is moving from county to county, then he's gonna hit either Tioga or Cortland County next."

A gravitational pull swelled inside David, the kind that made him want to stray from his home.

"Dave!" Jeff reeled him back in. "You there?"

"I'm listening." He turned his attention from the neighborhood, back to his best friend.

"This guy could hit Cortland County tonight. Keep your eyes open."

David scanned the neighborhood as that force yanked at his chest.

"Where the hell did she come from?" Jeff whispered, nodding toward a leggy brunette wearing a flowing skirt and a tight red top. The long, uncoordinated strides of her pale legs carried her up the driveway to the vacant house next door.

The force pulled harder, piercing David's sternum and hooking into his ribs, directing him to *her*. David locked eyes with the stranger as she limped barefoot toward the steps. Feelings of warning drowned in his attraction to her.

Jeff brushed shoulders with him. "I hope she's our new neighbor," he said, letting out a slow, breathy whistle. "Dibs."

"Dibs?" David's trance broke. "What is this, junior high?"

Despite talking big game, Jeff was far too much of a gentleman to ever lay claim to a woman. In high school, he wouldn't even approach his crush, who couldn't have made it more clear that she wanted him to ask her out. Whereas David—by the age of 18—had mastered the art of making women drop their panties with nothing more than a smoldering

25

stare. Over the years, Jeff worked on his confidence to approach women, but deep down, he was too much of a puppy. Especially for a woman like the one walking up the driveway next door.

Jeff smirked and then got serious. "Miss!" he called out.

The mysteriously charming woman climbed the steps without breaking David's gaze—there was no doubt in his mind that she wanted him.

"You okay?" Jeff shouted. "You injured?" He lowered his voice to a whisper. "Shoot, maybe I shouldn't have said that. What if she has a physical condition or something?"

As she reached the front door, it drifted open, and the gorgeous woman disappeared inside.

"Or maybe she's just rude." Jeff chuckled and poured more beer down his throat.

David released his breath, fighting the silent summoning from behind her closed doors. Plenty of experience taught him to be cautious of beautiful women—they were nothing but trouble. He had been knocked on his ass one too many times. Even his wife, who was the epitome of beauty, kicked him in the nads and left him squirming for mercy. She got paranoid, without any serious proof, then hopped in the sack with the first guy that made her feel special. To top it all off, she walked out on her family, claiming the appetite of a flesh and blood woman—whatever that meant—and leaving David to care for their teenage son.

"Dad!" Travis called from upstairs.

Jeff laughed. "That's him calling for attention."

"Don't start, man."

"Just saying you might have to take him outside every once in a while."

"I tried," David said with his hand on the doorknob. "He has no outdoor skills."

"Well maybe if you—"

"Lay off!" David snapped. "You don't know. Travis has no interest in anyone other than himself. I'm done trying to help that kid."

Travis's telescope was perched in the window of his second story bedroom. Gifted to him by his mother before she left, the telescope sat in a box for weeks, right next to the baseball bat that David had bought him.

"Finally decided to try that thing out, huh?" David asked as he stalled in the doorway, eyeing the untouched bat. It burned a little to know the kid chose the telescope over sports. Not that he was surprised. David had tried to teach the kid to play a couple years back—he'd always had a hell of a powerful swing—but it only resulted in strikeouts and foul balls. Every week for months, David made an unsuccessful attempt to practice with Travis. Tireless eye-rolls and huffs of derision wore David down, and he gave up on the kid. Only a year until graduation, so all David had to do was try not to screw the kid up too much.

"You gotta see this," Travis said.

David could not care less about looking through the eyepiece of the ex's guilt gift. The $300 shiny black stargazing piece of bribery that she had probably hoped would win Travis back. One hand on a warming beer, and the other in his pocket, David pretended to care and entered Travis's room.

"What are you looking at?" he asked, hovering over Travis's shoulder. His corner bedroom allowed a direct view into the backyard next door. The gorgeous woman in the fitted crimson top stood below, stretching her arms to the sky.

"Supermoon," Travis said. "It's rising now."

David lifted his eyes from the alluring brunette to see the full moon filling the gaps between the houses on the horizon. Of course. Travis was the only teenage boy he knew that would be looking at the moon instead of an insanely hot woman.

The woman's presence in the yard below lured David's attention away from the moon. Twilight turned the grass beneath her bare feet to a lifeless gray. Her flowing, knee-length skirt lifted in the breeze, allowing a flash of her bare thigh, and the gentle wind played in the strands of her hair.

Then, as if she knew exactly what David was thinking, she slid her shirt over her head.

David—needing to set an example for his kid—turned his back to her and dragged the telescope away from the window, fumbling like an idiot. "Whoa."

Travis's face, painted with confusion at first, turned stoic. "I wasn't looking at her. Honest."

David leaned the telescope against the wall. "What's weird about that, is I believe you."

He couldn't help but look again. Topless, she turned her body toward him—eyes lingering on the window for a moment

28

while he sank into the darkness of the room, hoping she didn't catch him gawking.

"Okay, so the neighbor's a nudist," David joked.

"When did she move in?" Travis asked.

David shrugged.

Travis moved his telescope from the wall, fiddling with the parts, while David stole another glimpse of *her*. A flutter in his chest caught his breath. The rest of her clothing had been removed. With her bare backside facing him, she greeted the rising moon in the east.

David forced himself away from the window again. "What's so super about a supermoon?"

"It's a bit closer to earth than usual, and it can look bigger sometimes," Travis said. "Especially when it rises."

David tried to combat his need to look again. Maybe if he were able to control his lustful desires, his wife would not have strayed to the bed of another man. If he had just looked away instead of enticing every gorgeous woman to bed with him, he would still have the one woman that ever meant anything to him. Perhaps if he loved her, and only her, the way she deserved to be loved—if he could have satisfied her needs emotionally— he might still have her. And perhaps Travis would still have a mother living with him.

"Can I set up my scope again now?"

"Go take a shower or something, Travis."

"But the moon's rising *now*," he argued.

"Now is clearly not a good time." David gestured out the window.

"Why should I have to suffer because of her?"

"You'll be asking yourself that about women for the rest of your life."

The compulsion within him to go to that stranger next door ebbed and flowed, but David remained mindful of the warning in his heart. He grabbed a fresh beer downstairs, avoiding the peep show—he had *some* class after all. And he had *some* desire to save his marriage, if his wife would ever take him back.

He stepped onto his front porch where Jeff was standing guard, as if the serial killer at-large would stroll into his neighborhood at any moment.

"Feels wrong not working."

"You said that already."

"I should go talk to her," Jeff said with a sly smile, "and let her know to keep her doors locked tonight. I gotta be a good neighbor and all."

"I wouldn't strike up a conversation now," David said. "She's naked in the backyard."

Jeff's eyes bulged. "You're full of shit."

"Nope," David said, and took another swig of beer. "But it's weird. She was staring at me through the window. Like she knew I was there and she didn't care."

"In the nude?" Jeff asked, brows furrowed.

"Yep."

"That's an invitation if I've ever heard of one," Jeff laughed.

David held his breath, considering the idea. "No. I'm off women for a while."

"That's no woman," Jeff smiled. "That's a goddess. You don't turn that down. If a woman like that is eye-screwing you, you offer her a drink."

David leaned on the post and sipped from his beer, withholding his lecherous thirst for the woman next door, along with the contrasting yearning for his wife's love. The warm summer breeze skimmed his arm hair as the force of *her* calling pulled at him again.

Jeff straightened up his stance, took a swig from his bottle, and tucked in his shirt. "If you're not going to talk to her, then I will."

"She's naked, man."

"I know that." Jeff cringed. "I'm not some perv. I'm gonna knock on her door, let her put some dang clothes on, and then introduce myself. Let her know she's safe in this neighborhood. Maybe I should put my uniform on. Women love that." He paused for a moment and shook his head. "No time for that. I gotta do this now while the mood is right."

Jeff strolled next door with his hands in the pockets of his cargo shorts, climbed the steps, and knocked.

After a few seconds, the door opened to the tall, enchanting woman—no longer naked, but draped in a red satin robe. The sight of her welcoming smile captivated David all the way from his porch. She turned away from Jeff and faced David's house, imprisoning his gaze again.

Then the unexpected—she turned back to Jeff and allowed him inside. The front door shut behind them. David kicked himself for not calling dibs on her first, but found comfort in knowing he did what seemed like the right thing.

As he headed upstairs, the intense sensation to go to her ceased. Released from her grasp, David stalled by Travis's room where the hiss of his shower grew louder. The moon crept higher against the darkening sky, spilling light through his window. Despite the trepidation within discouraging him from going to the window, David edged closer anyway, taking in the glow from the supermoon.

Travis's shower cut off.

David peered into the darkening yard below as Jeff and the woman stepped outside. With her back to David, she stood before Jeff's silhouetted frame in the moonlight and opened her robe to him. David leaned closer to the window, stunned. "What the hell?"

Jeff stood still—what a dumbass. A gorgeous woman in front of him, and he freezes. David would have known how to play her.

Jeff's arms dangled by his sides as she drifted closer. Pale hands slithered across his chest. David leaned against the frame of the window, drawn to her. She pushed Jeff to the ground with a violent jolt, and David jumped, ready to help his friend. But Jeff wasn't exactly fighting her off. He lay on the grass as she crawled over him.

That's when David should have turned away, but his eyes were trapped. The high contrast between her pale skin and dark shadows created an illusion of some inhuman form crawling with the awkward mechanics of an insect.

David squinted through the darkness trying to make sense of the contorted shape of her limbs.

Her robed body writhed and rocked over Jeff. David pulled his eyes away, toward the light beneath Travis's bathroom door to be sure his son wasn't coming. Despite his conscience insisting he look the other way, he was drawn back to the window.

Her back hunched over Jeff.

A darkness grew beneath them. A black shadow crept outward from under their bodies, so dark—like a void in the earth could swallow them whole.

The air shifted in the bedroom as Travis opened the bathroom door, stealing David's attention for only a moment.

The woman crouched over the growing black shadow. And Jeff was gone.

Her shoulders jerked in a violent, seizure-like episode. Still hovered over the black void, with her back to David, her head twisted in pulses as if being cranked by a wrench. The woman's eyes locked on him through the window. Impossible for her to see him through the darkened room, but her lips stretched into a sinuous smile inviting him to come to her.

Stumbling over Travis's books, David scrambled away from the window, unsure if his eyes were betraying him. All the possible explanations rushed through his mind. Weird lighting and shadows. Alcohol. An elaborate prank—knowing Jeff, it was the most likely of the scenarios.

"What happened?" Travis asked.

"Stay here," David urged. "Keep away from that window!"

The side yard, deep in the shadow of the house, provided cover while David went looking for Jeff. His heart hammered against his breastbone, bruising him from the inside, while he called for him.

"Jeff," he whispered as he stepped around the back of the house. Trying to remain calm and sensible, he walked into the moonlight, expecting Jeff to pop out of some hiding spot, laughing about how he "got him good."

"Jeff?" he called again.

While distracted by the nearly blinding light of the massive rising moon, he slipped. His foot slid in the grass, throwing off his balance, but he caught himself from falling.

"What the—"

Beneath his feet laid the black shadow where Jeff had been.

He knelt down and placed his fingertips in the dark, slick substance, then raised his hand to the moonlight. A red viscous fluid encased the tips of his fingers—blood.

His pulse sped faster than his icy blood could pump through his veins. David backed out of the carpet of bloody grass. Shaking hands pulled his phone out to call for help.

The woman in the red robe came out of her house with a grin. Moon glow reflected off her skin as she jerked toward him in convulsions that defied physics. The satin robe, open and draping from her breasts, exposed a long, rugged scar from her clavicle to pubis. A scar indicative of some horrible surgery, or some traumatic event that ripped her open from the base of her neck all the way down her body.

David's hands betrayed him as his finger dialed the last digit. The phone fell to the ground.

"911 dispatcher…" the woman's voice faded.

His throat swelled from the inside. He couldn't speak. Gravity pulled at his feet with so much force it felt like the earth would suck him in. Standing petrified, David's body was unresponsive to his desire to flee.

Her pale gray eyes, cratered with dark splotches, captivated him. Mesmerized and paralyzed, he allowed her closer. One delicate hand rested against his chest, radiating an energy that permeated his skin. It surged through his veins, swelling and receding.

"Luna," she said with a voice that hissed and rolled like ocean waves. "She's close tonight. So strong."

With a gentle nudge, she sent him falling backward. Joints fused stiff, David could not break his own fall as he crashed into the grass. Flat on his back, with his arms to his sides, lying only feet from the blanket of Jeff's blood, David struggled to escape his paralysis.

The woman opened her robe, exposing her body. The long, vertical strip of white scar tissue widened, splitting along the length of her torso.

"She must feed again." A gravely breath of pain and pleasure seeped from her parted lips.

The flesh at the scar's seam stretched and separated.

Long, white strands of fleshy tissue thickened and formed into spindly teeth. Unclasping from an interlocked position over her organs.

Ribs fractured. The newly formed monstrous fangs opened, exposing a cavernous abyss within her body.

Terror-ridden and charmed, David remained flat on the ground as she dropped to her hands and feet and scrambled over him.

Her eyes eclipsed to darkness.

The spiky teeth of her abdomen dripped saliva onto his belly, and a snarling moan rose from the beast within her gut. The fanged pit widened like the unhinging of a snake jaw, prepared to devour him.

Unable to close his eyes, he was forced to watch as it lunged upon him, delivering a fate he probably deserved.

A flash of Travis smiling. A glimpse of his wife dancing. The memory of his young son laughing hysterically after an epic swing of a wiffle-ball bat that busted the plastic ball in half. As the moments of his life filled his heart, David snapped back to reality as the beast screeched and jerked to the side.

Travis towered over him with the baseball bat on his shoulder.

It squirmed in the grass, squealing from the blow.

Travis heaved, trembling, panting. David—shocked by his son's bravery—shifted an arm beneath him. As his vision pulsed with his heartbeat, he tried to break from his petrified state to help Travis.

The woman's arms and legs buckled and snapped. She unfolded herself into an upright position.

David manipulated his numb legs and stood, but he could barely lift them to take a step.

Her blackened eyes revealed a glowing crescent as they came out of their eclipse. She moved toward Travis.

The atrocity in her belly hissed and drooled as it closed in on the boy.

"Travis!" David shouted, lunging his torpid body between them, knees weak, crumbling beneath the weight of his body.

The scream of a thousand voices howled from the creature, and police sirens joined in from down the street.

"You'll be all right," David said to his son as something caught his breath.

A pressure in his chest.

Travis's eyes widened with panic. A fleshy, bony tentacle exited David's sternum. The creature pierced him from behind and wrapped the segmented extension around his waist.

Travis struck at her abdomen again, cracking one of its teeth, as red and blue emergency lights flashed across the fencing.

"Over here!" Travis screamed for help.

The pale beast on all fours backed against the fence with David in tow. His son's image shrank as David was pulled into the shadows of the yard.

"Dad!" Travis called, but his voice was distant—safe.

Tingling numbness sparked through his circuits as David allowed the monster to take him far away. His body tore through the woods, dragged by the demon to be consumed later. Relief blanketed him, knowing that Travis was safe from the beast's appetite for flesh and blood.

THE GREAT AMERICAN ECLIPSE

A PRESSURE IN HELIA'S CHEST crushed her heart ever since her dad died. Every beat. Every breath. Every glimpse at the stars. "Keep looking up," he used to say.

Electric blue patches of sky peeked from behind towering pines as Helia and a friend hiked the trail to her dad's old research cabin. Dad loved setting up his telescope on the trail's clearing for some dark sky observing and often brought Helia along with him. But astronomy was only a hobby. By day, he studied fungi and parasites—lifespans and environments. Stardust and mold spores were all connected in some primordial way.

Nestled in the Adirondack Mountains and only a twenty minute hike to town, the cabin was a perfect location for researching rare fungi. And bonus, it sat in the path of totality for today's solar eclipse.

Free accommodations and college students—perfect match.

Musty cabin and sleeping on the floor—inconsequential factors.

"This is it," Helia said, turning off the dirt path, high-stepping onto the dewy forest floor. Her roommate Katie followed.

Shiny new solar panels adorned the cabin's weathered wooden roof. Parked near the front door, an ATV.

"Shit," Helia said under her breath, stopping short.

"What?" Katie asked.

"My Uncle Steve is here."

"Nooo…" Katie's mouth hung open. "The guy that—"

"Yeah, him…" Helia took a deep breath through her nose, mentally preparing herself for the interaction. She hadn't seen him since the funeral.

"What are you doing here?" Uncle Steve said, placing plastic sample baggies on the kitchen counter beside a microscope.

"What are *you* doing here?" Helia didn't hide the contempt in her tone.

"Field research. I do a lot of that now."

"You mean since you got fired?" She raised her eyebrows and crossed her arms.

40

Steve stuck his tongue in his cheek, clearly withholding a snappy comeback. Probably a good idea since he put on such a production at Dad's funeral. "I wasn't fired. I quit," he said through clenched teeth. "Something your dad should have done."

"You know what?" Helia's gut twisted. "This cabin belongs to my family, so why don't you just leave?"

Steve pulled the coffee pot from the maker and poured a cup. "I'm not going anywhere."

Katie edged closer. "Let's just drop off our stuff like we planned and go to town for the party."

"You here for the eclipse?" Uncle Steves's scruffy beard half-engulfed his coffee mug as he sipped.

"Yes," Katie answered.

Helia dropped her backpack. "We're hiking to town for the eclipse party. Maybe it's best you're not here when we get back."

"See the new solar panels?" Steve said. "I hooked the place up."

"Did you put in a toilet?" Katie crossed her legs.

Uncle Steve smiled and long laugh lines crinkled around his eyes. "Not yet. But..." He gestured toward the window. "...nature is my bathroom. You know, you can view the eclipse from the hiking trail right out there. That's what I plan to do. You don't have to go back to town."

Helia bit her tongue. So many foul replies whizzed through her mind.

Katie side-eyed her. "But there's no party or booze on the hiking trail, is there?"

"Holy shit. Are you twenty-one already?" Steve turned on the nineteen-inch tube TV and adjusted its foil-wrapped rabbit ears.

Helia nodded. She wanted to tell him *yes,* that she partied with friends last month for her birthday. She wanted to remind him of the good times she used to have with him and Dad, camping and researching parasites and fungi and bacteria. She wanted to know what her uncle was working on today. But mostly, she wanted to stay mad at Uncle Steve for saying such terrible things about his own brother at the funeral.

"That's some ancient technology." Katie pinched her fingers around the TV antenna. "What is it, from the 80s or something?"

"It works," Steve smiled. "That's all I need. Mexico will be reaching totality in a little while. Let's see what's happening."

On a static-ridden screen, an anchorwoman in a yellow pantsuit announced, "Today, most of the United States will be able to view at least a partial solar eclipse. For the few who are lucky enough to be in the path of totality—or determined enough to get there—a rare, spectacular reward awaits. Total solar eclipse. Donald Harris is outside the studio now."

The TV cut to a middle-aged man. "Wear protective eyewear when looking at the sun, or you could go blind." He opened a small pouch and removed a pair of cardboard solar glasses. "For better protection and to enhance your viewing

42

experience, be sure to check for the new certification from VSTAC—"

"Bullshit!" Uncle Steve slammed his coffee mug on the wobbling kitchen table.

Donald Harris held the glasses up to the camera. "VSTAC certified glasses are guaranteed to allow in an extra wavelength of light while still protecting your eyesight."

Uncle Steve scratched his beard. "That doesn't even make sense."

Helia's dad and Uncle Steve had worked together at VSTAC in parasitology. Back before Dad's promotion. The multi-billion dollar corporation produced pesticides mostly, recently expanding their research into solar energy and even optics for astronomy. Uncle Steve had bad blood with VSTAC.

"Back to you Yang," Donald Harris said.

Yang smiled. "These new and improved glasses have very fragile film that shouldn't be left out of their pouch for more than about an hour or so, which is enough time to view the eclipse. Prolonged exposure to air can damage the film and cause blindness. So, don't open them until it's eclipse time."

"How in the fuck is that safer than the regular ISO certification? Solar glasses have been fine for years," Steve said. "Now some new VSTAC certification is required. Why? VSTAC didn't even get into optics beyond microscope development until a few years ago."

Katie squirmed, obviously needing to use a bathroom. "If the glasses don't last that long, then why is everyone saying we should use them?"

"Because some money-grubbing asshole told some schmuck in a lab that he should go against all ethics and tell the public they're worth it," Uncle Steve said.

"And by schmuck, do you mean my dad?"

Uncle Steve sighed. His shoulders dropped. "Helia, I have no beef with you."

"Well I have a beef with *you*." She turned away and glared out the window.

Katie edged toward the door. "I'm going to find a place to use the bathroom." She snuck out before Helia could beg to go with her.

"Well go ahead," Steve leaned against the counter, facing Helia. "Let me have it."

Helia whipped around. "I hate you." Her breath hitched, shocked that she said it aloud. "I hate that you got drunk at my dad's funeral. I hate that you said all those awful things. I hate that you're an insufferable conspiracy theorist. I mean, get a life!" She couldn't stop the deluge of tears. There was no hiding them at this point. But the exodus of feelings felt so good. "You couldn't handle the fact that my dad got the security clearance for the VSTAC research and you didn't. You're a jealous man. You're a liar. And I hate you."

Instead of fighting back, Steve went to a closet and pulled out a black bag. The small camera-style bag dangled by the strap as Steve held it out to her.

"What's this?" She made sure to keep her tongue sharp while she wiped her tears away.

"It was your dad's."

She unzipped the bag and pulled out a set of binoculars.

"The binoculars of an astronomer," Steve said. "Zeiss 20 by 60 image-stabilizing binos. Your dad always specified he was only an amateur astronomer, but he was practically an expert on solar dynamics and optics for observing the sun. That's why he got the clearance. He was the most qualified for the job."

Helia allowed her fingers to run along the binoculars focuser where her father's hands used to touch. "What job?"

"I don't know, exactly."

"Then why were you so mad at him?"

Steve shrugged. "He used those binos to view the last eclipse."

"I remember. I watched that one with him. We drove to South Carolina to view it." Digging into the bag, Helia found the solar lenses to fit over the end of the binoculars, as well as a plastic pair of eclipse eyeglasses in a side pocket.

"Thought you should have it," Steve said. "Keep looking up."

Helia sniffled. "That's what dad used to say."

"I know."

Katie returned. "I thought you weren't supposed to use a telescope or binoculars to view the eclipse."

Helia put the round filters on the end of the binoculars. "If you have the right filters, it's okay."

Katie pulled a mylar pouch from her backpack and held it up. She had picked up two pairs the day before. One for each of them. "But these are supposed to be better. The news and the people at the distribution center said so."

"Your dad's solar glasses and the bino filters are fine for viewing the eclipse. They're both ISO certified. Probably even better than those new glasses. There's something weird about those things."

"Come on, Uncle Steve!" Helia threw her arms up. "There's nothing wrong with them. You're just mad they were made by VSTAC."

Steve looked to the ceiling and balled his fists. "There are things you don't know."

"Let's go, Katie." Helia slung the bag over her shoulder and left before she screamed at her delusional uncle again.

As they headed down the trail toward town, a large group of people with bright-colored clothes—like they came straight from a department store catalogue—hiked up the mountain. Eight people, adults and children, smiling, laughing, headed toward the summit.

Helia and Katie followed the trail down to the open stretch of land that her dad used to call Stargazer's Knob. The rounded hilltop overlooked the outskirts of Old Forge. The viewing party came into sight about a hundred yards down the hill. Guitars twanged. White squares dotted the field. Beer and wine tents awaited. Crowds of tiny, far-away people stared at the sun through cardboard, solar-filtered glasses, awaiting its start at 1:11 p.m.

"This is a nice spot up here," Helia said, enjoying the open expanse and seclusion. "I could hang out here all day."

"But not without beer," Katie laughed.

"Let's go get a few beers and come back," Helia said.

After the descent through the woods, they arrived at 12:45 p.m. A field littered with people lounging on their backs. Kids looking to the sky with VSTAC cardboard solar glasses pressed to their faces. Plastic cups spilled dribbles of beer onto the grass as inebriated people navigated the crowds. Folks rubbed their eyes—probably because they were staring at the sun naked-eye.

Hundreds of people had come to the small mountain town to observe. A group of local astronomers, with telescopes aimed at the sun, sat under umbrella shades.

"Free VSTAC solar glasses!" One of them shouted.

Helia approached. "So, what do you think of these VSTAC glasses? Are they really better?"

A balding man stood beside a small solar telescope. "I think they're *free*. So why not?"

Another man chimed in. "A lot of hype over glasses that aren't any better than what we already have. But, you can't beat free… Want a pair?"

Helia shook her head as Katie ripped open her mylar pouch and pulled out the VSTAC cardboard glasses. She pressed them to her eyes and looked toward the sun.

"We have about five more minutes before first contact," the astronomer said. "That's when the moon first makes its appearance at the edge of the sun."

"It's just a boring white circle right now." Katie's face glowed in the sunlight. She removed the glasses and rubbed her right eye.

"You okay?" Helia asked.

"I think I got something in my eye." She fluttered her eyelashes so as not to disturb her thick mascara. "Shit. It burns." Katie wiped the edge of her eye with her finger.

A local country band rocked the main stage.

"This party sucks," Katie said, blinking.

"I might go back up to the Knob."

"Beer first," Katie rubbed her eye again. "I'm going to run to the bathroom to rinse out my eye. You get beer."

As Helia waited in line, time of first contact approached. At 1:09 p.m. all heads on the field turned to the sky.

Helia pulled out her dad's plastic pair of solar glasses. At 1:11, she lifted her protected eyes to a small white disc against a black backdrop. The moon chomped a black nick off the edge of the sun. Only 0.001% of the sun's light made it through her glasses, but it burned an imprint into her memory that would never fade.

An undulating sound of elation moved through the crowd.

"I see it!" Voices erupted. "Do you see it?"

Another hour until totality, so Helia removed her glasses and wandered the crowd, looking for Katie by the bathroom. By the beer tent. She couldn't find her.

She passed a man with a walking cane and guide dog by his side. The blind man smiled with his face to the sky, ready to enjoy totality with his other senses.

A nasal voice from a group of people behind her grabbed Helia's attention. "Texas just had totality, and a group of people lost their minds like it was the Rapture or something."

"Crazy doomsdayers," another voice said.

Helia huffed and looked around the crowd wondering if any insane, end-of-world losers lurked among them.

She texted Katie: *Did you see first contact?*

Yeah. I'm at the first aid tent for my eye.

You ok? Helia asked.

They're telling everyone to stop staring at the sun with no eye protection. I was wearing the glasses, asshats.

I'll come sit with you, Helia offered.

No. Go watch the damn eclipse. This is your thing. I'll meet you at the knob when I'm done.

The seclusion called to Helia. She slipped away with two beers and climbed the hill through the woods until she reached the clearing that overlooked the party.

She lay on her back, hands tucked behind her head, enjoying the distant music in peace. Periodically, she slipped on her dad's solar glasses, or used the solar-filtered binoculars to view the partial eclipse as the moon obscured more of the sun.

Katie checked in with a text every few minutes to let her know she was still waiting. People were pouring into the first aid tent with irritated eyes. It had to have been the glasses, somehow. VSTAC was pretty pushy about the new certification.

Her mind drifted to her dad, and the long hours leading up to his death. The sweat seeping through his clothes when he'd get home. He was nervous. Paranoid about something. The

49

thought slipped into her mind that maybe her dad was involved in the making of these glasses. Maybe he knew they'd hurt people... but he worked in the bio-tech department, not in the optical field. They weren't even in the same building as far as she knew.

Announcements sounded from below that the time of the total eclipse was drawing near. A crescent of sunlight remained.

You're missing it! She texted Katie.

Minutes later, a sliver.

Then a slim white line. Shadows of her arm against the blanket revealed crisp lines, individual hairs. The diamond ring—the ring of sunlight with the last gem of light.

Then darkness. Total solar eclipse.

The crowd below released a conglomeration of moans, oohs, and cheers. A sound of joy and awe hit Helia's soul like a shockwave. She removed her dad's solar glasses to view the eclipse naked-eye. The solar corona stretched out with strands of feathery light against a dark, purple-gray sky. Pink-orange glow on the horizons all around.

Venus. Jupiter. Saturn. The bright star Capella...

Darkness surrounded her, but light filled her heart.

Goosebumps prickled her arms as the temperature dropped. Three squirrels scurried across the clearing into the trees. Birds flew back to the tree canopy.

"I'll keep looking up, Dad," she whispered, then placed an ardent kiss upon her fingertips and raised them to the sky.

Down the hill at the party, masses of people dropped their belongings. Hundreds of them, all at once, froze.

The diamond ring returned. No cheers or eruptions from the crowd. They all began to stagger around, aimlessly.

Did you see it? What's going on? Helia texted.

No reply.

The moon's shadow moved, returning a flood of sunlight.

Silence below and an empty field with only a handful of people left behind. "Where'd they all go?" she whispered. Garbage, lawn chairs, and even baby strollers were left behind.

I'm coming down there to get you, she texted.

Few people remained. Katie should be easy to find. After removing the solar filters from the binoculars, she slowly scanned the field for her friend.

First in her field of view was the blind man. He rose from his chair with his dog by his side. A burly man in a white button-down shirt approached him.

Helia pushed her image-stabilizing button on her dad's binoculars, and the view of the guide dog steadied. In a threatened stance, the dog lowered his head, then cowardly darted away from his owner. While swinging his walking cane, the blind man backed away as the man in the white shirt hunched over.

Her field of view swept across the party field to another person.

"Katie!" Helia called out, realizing there's no way she'd hear her from up there. Eyes back to the binoculars, she zoomed in on Katie, standing beside a child in a stroller.

Returning to the view of the blind man—he had fallen on his backside. The man in white stood over him, hunching like he'd vomit. His spine swelled through his white shirt. A ridge pulsed along his spinal column.

"What the fuck?"

She pulled her eyes away from the binos as if they could be lying to her, then looked again. A black, shiny appendage telescoped out from the back of the man's neck. It extended over his head. The pointed tip of the spider-like leg stretched toward the blind man.

With a swift, calculated jab, the antenna pierced his eye.

Helia gasped—her feet locked to the ground with paralyzing fear. Binoculars slid in her sweaty grip as she scanned to find her friend again.

Katie bent over a child in the umbrella stroller. A similar hunched spine along Katie's back. Pulsing. Then the same type of appendage ejected from Katie, injecting into the stroller. Tiny toddler-sized legs trembled.

Helia considered for a moment rushing down there to find out what was going on. To help her friend, and the blind man and the baby. But instead, heroic intentions fled. Not considering why or what was happening, she ran. Feet pounding the ground. One after the other, back up the mountainside. Concentrating solely on getting far away.

A rumble of an engine cut through the forest ahead, and her body instinctively dove off-trail, hiding in a patch of thorny brush. Skin pricked and bleeding, she quieted herself as the rumbling ATV approached. Uncle Steve.

Scrambling out of the brush, waving her hands, she called for him as he nearly sped past her.

"The news," he said, bringing the four-wheeler to a stop. "Austin, Texas. Indianapolis ... Is it here too? Where's Katie?"

Opening her mouth to speak proved to be futile. Unable to gather her thoughts to explain what she had seen, her jaw simply hung open. Her brain couldn't process the events into any sort of emotion, so no tears fell. Adrenaline, or maybe fear, kept her from crying.

"Do we need to go get her?" Steve asked. His voice was distant, like he was calling to her from inside a deep cave.

Helia shook her head and climbed onto the back of his ATV.

Steve called over his shoulder. "People are infected with something." He paused as the ATV bumped over large roots across the trail. "What happened down in town?"

He cut a sharp corner onto an overgrown trail and pulled up to the cabin.

Inside, Helia paced, waiting for an incoming threat, but there was nothing.

"This cabin is pretty well-camouflaged here," Uncle Steve said. "We can see the hikers way out there on the main trail, but they can't see the cabin unless they look hard enough."

The reporters were on the television set. Co-anchor Donald Harris sat in the studio, sweating through his cheap suit, puffy-faced, and sickly. Static stripes broke up the reception. Media clips from across the country played on screen. Entire masses of eclipse-watchers dropped everything like a horde of zombies.

"That happened here!" Helia said.

"That's not the weirdest part," Uncle Steve said. "Keep watching."

Captivated by the screen, there was no other option but to watch. From Texas, a blurred video revealed a dark mass flash before the camera. When the clip paused, the mass took shape as something with long, spindly legs and antenna.

"What is that?" Helia asked.

Uncle Steve shook his head. "Too blurry to tell. Hoping it's a fake."

"It's not fake," Helia said. "That antenna thing came out of Katie."

"What do you mean, it came out of Katie? Those things are *inside* people?"

Helia locked on the television screen, hoping for answers, but Allison Yang delivered nothing but speculation. "This solar eclipse must have had an effect on people. Driving them to madness, turning them into these things."

"That's impossible," Helia yelled to the woman on screen.

Yang continued. "Donald, you viewed the eclipse and you're not looking so good. Maybe you need to see the doctor…"

Donald stared at the camera, sweating and silent.

"It doesn't make sense," Helia said. She explained everything to her uncle. The blind man, the baby, Katie.

"Parasite?" Uncle Steve said.

"What kind of parasite can infect people like that? How?" Helia returned to the window. "Bioterrorism with parasites? Is that even possible?"

Uncle Steve lingered by the television set, rubbing his beard as if answers would pop out of it.

"How do you infect the entire country with a parasite using the eclipse?" Helia asked.

"You can't." Uncle Steve says. "That's stupid. You can't infect photons," he laughed with a hint of derision. "We're not infected. We both viewed the eclipse. It's some other common factor."

"The glasses. The VSTAC glasses," Helia said.

"Exactly. Do you have a pair?"

Helia dug into her backpack and pulled out the glasses Katie had picked up the day before. She handed the mylar pouch to her uncle.

"VSTAC certified to infect the population." He pinched the corner of the pouch and held it before himself. "And individually wrapped to preserve a parasite."

"What? Why would anyone do that?" Helia asked.

"Millions of people across the US viewed the eclipse today," Uncle Steve said, "being coerced into using these specific VSTAC certified glasses for viewing. Everyone that wore them got infected."

"But why?"

Uncle Steve shook his head.

"We need to call someone," Helia said.

"There's no cell tower within reach. If I need anything, I have to drive into town."

"I know." Helia sighed, sitting down at the table with her head in her hands. "It was him, wasn't it?"

Steve dropped the VSTAC glasses into a sample baggie. "Who?"

"Dad. This was what he was working on wasn't it? This was the big secret thing."

"We don't know that." Steve pulled a large roll of heavy plastic from the cabinet beneath his microscope and sighed.

"But you were thinking it. What do you know, Uncle Steve?"

"He was working with optics but he wouldn't say why. It was classified. I pushed for info, but he dodged the topic. He was acting so weird. Said he wanted out, but it was too late. I tried to tell him he could walk away from whatever it was, but he wouldn't. He said he was in too deep. Ethics didn't matter anymore. All sorts of bullshit."

"He was so scared." Helia's voice trembled. "Dad looked guilty. All week leading up to his death. Like when he accidentally ran over my cat Muffin with the car. Shaking and fidgeting, and stammering. He didn't die in a car accident, did he? He was going to tell someone about whatever VSTAC was up to with these glasses, and he was murdered!" Tears streamed down her cheeks.

Steve stood silent, dumbfounded. "I'm sorry about how I acted at the funeral."

Helia caught her breath between sobs and shrugged her shoulders. What did it matter anymore?

"Let's examine these glasses to see what we're dealing with," Uncle Steve said.

He hung plastic from the ceiling to floor, closing off an area around his microscope. "It's not a real clean-room situation, but it's the best we can do with what we have."

The clear plastic sheeting allowed her to watch from outside the makeshift room. With gloved hands, a ventilation mask, and a pair of tweezers, Steve set the glasses onto the microscope.

Helia released a held breath and used her sleeve to dry up her face.

After a cursory naked-eye inspection, Steve excised a small sample of the solar film from the glasses and placed it on a microscope slide.

"There's a strange surface texture," he said with his face to the eyepiece. "Lumpy or something. This material is so dark, I need more light on it." After positioning a lamp near the sample, he flicked the switch and flooded the slide with light. "Very bumpy. This isn't typical solar film… wait a minute."

"What is it?"

With eyes to the microscope, Steve said, "Definitely an organism. Larva. Planktonic like trochophore, but not really. Cilia-like structures. Hellgrammite-ish."

"I don't know what you're saying!"

"I'm saying I don't know what it is. I've never seen this before." He turned to face her through the plastic. "I've seen everything. Even undiscovered organisms look like already-discovered organisms. This structure is differ—!" He jumped from the microscope, knocking over his rolling stool.

"What?"

"It jumped!" He threw open a drawer, ripping it from the tracks. It fell to the floor in his excitement.

"What do you mean, it jumped?"

Uncle Steve dug through the fallen equipment on the floor and grabbed a hefty sample bag. He used the tweezers to reach for the slide. "It grew."

"It grew?"

"Yes," he yelled. "It grew. It was microscopic, now I can see it naked-eye."

Thin silver tweezers pinched at a tiny thing under the microscope light and Steve held it up to the heat lamp. Helia pressed her face against the plastic, breath fogging her view. She moved to the opening to get a better look.

A worm-like thing, shorter than her pinky-nail squirmed between the pincers. Beneath the hot light, it swelled, stretched, and convulsed.

"It's still growing. The heat wakes up the dormant larva," Steve said.

Uncle Steve, with surgical precision, slid the organism into the sample bag, tweezers and all, then sealed it. Separately, he bagged the glasses and the foil pouch they came in.

Leaving his protective gear in the plastic room, he came out. "We're at risk for contamination," Uncle Steve warned. "We should stay here to prevent contamination to the public... but the whole damn country is already contaminated, so fuck that. We need to leave."

"Shhh." Blotches of colorful clothing moved beyond the trees, out on the main trail. "Hikers coming down from the top," Helia whispered. Using her binoculars, she spied on them.

The same laughing group that passed by on the trail earlier. Single file, they lurched through the woods. Twitching, convulsing, they lumbered down the mountain.

"Infected?" Helia asked. "Maybe we're at higher risk of contamination out there than we are in here."

Uncle Steve faced the television. His ominous voice drained all remaining hope. "It doesn't look like there's anywhere to go anyway."

On screen, Allison Yang was poorly lit by studio lights. Donald, green and clammy, sat halfway off screen.

"I apologize for the quality," Allison said, crying. "Our crew is gone. They're all gone. We have new footage from social media."

Allison moved off screen and switched the feed to a video of the White House grounds. On the famous South Lawn, creatures gathered. Black and gray shimmering bodies. Clumps of long, crustaceous legs from torso to abdomen, moved too fast to count them. Along their dorsal plate, a spinal ridge extended in an arched antenna over their heads.

Feed cut to a clip from Dover Air Force Base, where the creatures assembled in hangars.

At U.S. Naval Station Norfolk in Virginia, they lurked in groups upon the flight decks of aircraft carriers.

"How?" Helia asked. "That's not even in the path of totality.

"They had a partial eclipse all over the country." Steve sat in a chair and held a hand over his mouth.

Through the tiny tube television, the entire country crumbled before them. Helpless, as the monsters trapped people on the street. A mother pulled from her child, screaming. Pointed antennae injected into her terrified eyes as her child ran. Once injected, the infected mother tremored and collapsed to the ground. Then she stood, and moved on as if nothing had happened.

Yang's somber voice spoke through the clips. "There are thousands of these videos."

Helia's chest heaved with nervous breaths.

"How long have they been planning this attack?" she asked. "VSTAC. The factories that made them. Who orchestrated this? What role would my dad have played?"

Uncle Steve's eyes went glassy. "If... and I mean this as a big *if*... If your dad had a role in this, he would have been involved in developing the right conditions for the parasite to survive in a dormant state... That could be why they wanted him so badly. He was an expert on parasitic hosts, environments, but also knew a lot about solar filters."

"Jesus... He wouldn't have."

Leaning forward in his chair, Uncle Steve's color drained from his face.

"Uncle Steve. He wouldn't. Would he?"

Yang came back on the screen as Helia's gut twisted. "It's 6:45 p.m. and..." she looked to her co-anchor. "Snap out of it Donald. Please."

Donald sat in full view of the camera under the bright lights, skin dehydrated, stretched and cracked. Eye sockets sunken in. His face morphed and stretched. Coarse skin cracked along the eyelid, then down the nose, forming a crevice from eye to mouth. Yang screamed and staggered out of view.

Black and gray iridescence exposed beneath the surface of his broken face.

Donald's body burst open—cracked from head to belly. Human halves peeled off of him like a caterpillar shedding its skin, exposing the creature beneath. Fully grown.

Helia squealed.

Screaming backstage faded. A studio door slammed.

Then a static, not from the poor reception of the television, but something coming from the creature. A whispering, mechanical, clicking hum. It moved off-screen, leaving an empty, silent studio.

Helia covered her mouth in shock. Barely able to control her shaking body, she managed to speak through chattering teeth. "The parasite turns people into that? Is that what's in that sample bag? Is that what came out of Katie?"

Uncle Steve edged closer to the screen. "I think it's a parasitoid. They feed off the host until they're big enough and strong enough to live on their own." Uncle Steve's face seemed to light up with scientific wonder. "Question is, did it evolve here on Earth, or—"

"Don't say it." Helia's gut churned at the notion of some alien invasion. The queasiness couldn't be ignored any longer. She rushed outside to vomit. The rustling leaves overhead whispered like a static, evoking the memory of the creature from the studio. A chill cut through her body so sharp it could've sliced her in half like anchorman Donald Harris.

When she returned inside, Uncle Steve was behind the plastic sheet again, studying the organism. "It's dead. At least it looks dead. With no host, and no safe place to lay dormant, like the film in the glasses, it can't survive, and can't grow beyond the larval stage."

"What do we do now?" Helia asked. "Where can we go?"

Ideas for finding refuge ran thin. Nowhere in the United States was safe, as every state could have been exposed. Getting out of the country entirely would be ideal. A boat—cross the ocean? Perhaps if they get far enough away on land... The further they could get away from the line of totality, toward the areas that had only partial eclipse-viewing, fewer people should have been infected. Fewer people watched in the far south of the country.

"Florida?"

"That's a hell of a hike." Steve dug out an old Rand McNally map of the United States from a drawer.

"Do you think we can make it?" Helia asked.

Uncle Steve shrugged. "We don't have enough food or water to stay here."

A knock at the door startled them both to a standing position.

"Help!" A man yelled. "Help me!"

"What if it's a trick," she silently mouthed her words, desperate for her uncle to ignore the man.

"Help!" He pounded at the door.

Uncle Steve opened and let him in. A man, frantic and covered in fresh dirt and scratches, poured into the cabin.

"They're after me," he panted, darting straight to the window. His pressed shirt untucked and torn at the sleeve. "I don't know what they are. They got my family. I've been running off-trail for hours. We have to get to town and get help."

"There *is* no help," Uncle Steve said and pointed to the empty news studio on the television.

The man backed into the corner with his hands over his mouth. "You've seen them? Are they in town too?"

"They're everywhere," Helia said. "The whole country." The weight of her words had a physical effect on her body. A pressure deep inside hurt when she inhaled. A pressure more crushing than the weight of her father's death.

As daylight failed, Helia studied the map of the mountains and the trails leading to the Appalachian Trail. A trek to Florida would take weeks, the Pacific Northwest, even longer. And with no wilderness skills, her confidence in surviving waned.

A scratch on the side of the cabin jerked her to attention.

The man—the stranger, whose name she never asked— groaned at the sound. His eyes widened.

Uncle Steve grabbed Helia's wrist and dragged her behind the plastic sheet. Opening the lower cabinet, he whispered, "Hide."

"Where can I hide?" The man followed Uncle Steve behind the plastic.

"You and I aren't going to fit down there," he said, closing Helia inside.

Her surroundings went black with the click of the closing door. Knees bumping against her chin, she trembled. Her heavy breathing was loud enough to give away her location.

"Don't come out," he told her through the wood. "No matter what."

The scratching along the cabin walls amplified inside of the cramped, musty cabinet. Helia cracked the door and peeked out.

"Grab something to fight with," Uncle Steve said, lifting the wood-cutter's axe from the wall.

"I'm running for it," the man said. "I'm leaving."

Steve charged toward the cabinet and kicked it shut, leaving Helia in the dark again.

Stomping feet vibrated the floorboards.

The plastic sheet ruffled. Glass shattered.

"You idiot!" Steve shouted.

The stranger's mournful shriek seeped through the cabin walls. It lasted but a fraction of a second.

The sudden silence dried her mouth.

"Uncle Steve," Helia whispered. She cracked the cabinet door. Her uncle sat at the table. An axe in his right hand. His shaking hand poured a shot of whiskey, then took a swig. From across the dank room, through the plastic, their eyes met.

Something moved beyond Helia's field of view.

Bits of glass crunched near the window.

Static—but not the electric snow of the television. Something organic and alive, echoing off the rustic beams of the cabin walls. A breathy, guttural static.

The black and gray shimmering creature approached Uncle Steve, who remained still at the table, adjusting his grip on the axe.

The spinal ridge of the creature throbbed as the long appendage telescoped out of its back, and over its head. The humming static from the beast intensified as the tip of its appendage formed a moist droplet. Inside that droplet, the incipient, larval stage of the apocalypse squirmed.

Uncle Steve, in a swift motion, spun out of his seat and swung the axe at the creature's thorax. His weapon bounced off of the exoskeleton and flung across the room against the cabinet, closing Helia inside, and obscuring her view.

Static clicked and echoed, vibrating the wood of the cabinet.

The hefty thud of his body collapsing to the floor reverberated through the cabinet walls.

Containing her pain and fury, Helia held her screams inside. Eyes squeezed shut. Face soaked with tears. Spit strung from lip to lip, she tried to quell the chattering of her teeth.

Glass crunched. Footsteps—Uncle Steve. But it wasn't really him anymore.

The front door creaked open and the cabin was silent again.

Uncertain how much time had passed since Steve infected, and the creature left, Helia stayed in the confines of the cabinet. Five hours could have passed—or perhaps only five minutes.

Helia pushed on the cabinet door and fell onto the floor, eyes closed, waiting for one of them to take her, but she was alone.

Fumbling through the dark cabin, she packed her bag with the map and a few supplies, then climbed onto the ATV. Starting the engine may draw them in, but she wasn't confident she could outrun them on foot either.

"Just go," she whispered. The engine roared. Dirt kicked up behind her as she tore away from the cabin out to the main trail.

Heart thrashing within her ribcage, she focused on moving forward with a terror so intense her heart could have stopped beating. In a way, she wished it would.

She cut up the mountain trail, away from town, with only starlight to guide her.

Static-like noise loomed overhead, but Helia pushed on, hoping the rustling of tree leaves was to blame for the sound. Several minutes up the mountain, she noticed she was only a millimeter to empty on the gas gauge.

"Shit."

She reached the observation tower and cut the engine. A thicket of brush made decent cover for the four-wheeler. Helia ran up the steps to the observation deck at the top.

Thunderous booms roared in the distance.

Explosions. It was all falling apart. Patches of horizon glowed orange from destruction.

Helia crouched down in the corner of the observation tower, certain one of those creatures followed. Or perhaps they'd all moved out of the woods, on to the cities and towns.

She waited for the noise. The living, breathing static, but only heard the friction of leaves in the wind.

Another boom from behind her, miles away, startled her. She whipped her head around looking for them. She could swear she could feel them, over her shoulder, waiting to pierce her eye, but there was nothing there. The stairs down were black and empty as she listened for that static.

Her heart broke, awaiting her inevitable demise, but she couldn't bear to see it coming. She couldn't bear to look down at the dying world any longer.

Starlight pierced the black sky above. Bright pinpoints of tranquil light reached out to Helia and grabbed hold. A world of destruction unfolded beyond the mountains, and a looming threat could have been climbing the stairs at that very moment for all she knew.

Static was everywhere. In the trees. In the sound of her panicked breaths.

Unable to accept any of it, she locked her gaze on the peaceful dome of starlight above.

"Keep looking up," she whispered with tears blurring the stars into blobs.

"Keep looking up."

"Keep looking up."

BEST SEAT IN THE HOUSE

100-word drabble

A MUFFLED VOICE ANNOUNCED, "Ring Master!"

The crowd cheered.

Poverty kept kids like me outside, so through a small hole, I stole a sparkle-eyed glimpse of the man in red coattails. His dark, hollow eyes gripped me. A sinuous smile, outlined with scarlet lips, opened to a cavernous blackness.

In the stands, the townspeople stood paralyzed.

Ring Master pulled in a breath. Particles in the air illuminated as they were sucked in. The audience's mouths opened wide, as life made an exodus from their bodies, breathing energy into *him*.

Ring Master glowed, then looked in my direction. "Somebody hasn't paid."

ABANDONED SOULS

THERE WAS NO SIGNAL at the new house. Bundled in her dad's Navy sweatshirt, Brooke sat outside of the townhome fiddling with her phone. An icy breeze lashed against the naked trees in the desolate military housing community. A crunchy brown leaf clung for dear life to the branch above while she scanned the neighborhood of vacant driveways and overgrown lawns. She arrived so late last night she couldn't remember getting out of the car and walking into the house.

I can't believe Dad ditched me in this crap hole.

A playground sat at the end of the street. Three kids stood behind a short plastic wall on a platform. Brooke stepped off the porch and headed toward the sidewalk to get a better look. They weren't playing. The kids whispered among themselves and delivered grim stares in Brooke's direction.

Weirdos.

Movement in the window next door caught Brooke's attention. A pale face backed away from the window upstairs. The curtains shut.

Weirdos everywhere.

Wind bellowed between the townhouses. The chill of the November air bit her face, but Brooke would rather bare it than go inside. Her stepmom Mandy was in there drowning herself in a box of merlot as usual. Their household goods hadn't arrived by truck yet, so it's not like she had anything to unpack to keep her busy. All morning, Mandy had sat in the corner with her wine, drinking and taking selfies.

Why her father married such a mindless twit was beyond comprehension. However, Brooke wondered if it was so he'd have a live-in babysitter after Mom had left. Whatever the reason, it didn't matter. Countless deployments left Brooke under the care of an idiot, and this forced her to be incredibly self-reliant. In another year and a half, Brooke would be old enough to move out. By that time, Dad would be retiring and wanting his freedom anyway.

Good riddance.

The tallest boy of the three on the playground waved his hand to summon Brooke. There was nothing else to do on this base, so Brooke adjusted her hood and headed over. She climbed the ladder and joined the three in the small elevated cove.

"Hey," Brooke said.

"I'm Hunter," the oldest one said. His dark hair poked out from under his beanie. "This is Karrie." He put his hand on a young girl who couldn't have been more than six. "And this is Danny." A boy about ten years old picked at a string on his mittens.

"Brooke," she introduced herself. "Are you their brother?"

"No. What we're about to tell you never leaves this place." Hunter's grave expression was unfaltering. He sat down on the platform in the playground hideout. The small kids sat on each side of him and Brooke joined them.

She smirked and fought to keep from laughing aloud, awaiting a joke. Their faces were solemn and desperate. Karrie sat with her legs folded, leaning against Hunter. The boy was wide-eyed and peeking over his shoulder toward the street.

"I've been looking after Karrie and Danny since they got here last week . . . at least until their parents come back."

"They're not coming back!" Danny said.

"You don't know that." Karrie furrowed her brow.

"We've been left here." Danny hung his head and drew imaginary pictures on the platform with his finger.

Hunter shook his head. "All we know is that we have to look out for each other."

"What do you mean?" Brooke raised an eyebrow.

"They were taken," he said.

"Who?"

"The kids." Hunter peeked over the top of the playground wall. "Kids that come here go missing. Some parents too. And it's like nobody knows or cares. This place isn't a base."

74

Brooke scrunched up her face. "What is this, some live action role playing thing?"

"Someone is taking the kids." Hunter whispered.

"What are you talking about?"

"Look around," Hunter said. "All the empty houses. The school, the commissary, the exchange—it's all closed."

"And kids are being taken?" Brooke asked in a tone laced with skepticism.

"It's the creeper MPs," Karrie whispered. "They take them to the bad place and eat their souls."

"So, like soul-sucking vampires? Cute!" Brooke laughed, but nobody else did.

Brooke stood up. "I think I'm good. I'll catch you guys—"

"They usually come at night," Hunter interrupted, "only at night, and take kids from their houses."

The cold air bit at Brooke's nose and fingertips as the wind picked up again. She backed up to the ladder.

Hunter continued. "They take them to that old firing range down in the woods. We don't know what happens to them after that though."

"Tell her about the hole!" Danny said.

Hunter shushed him. "We hide at night, so we don't get taken. We keep each other safe. I've been here for three weeks, and I've been able to dodge them. Stick with me, and we'll keep each other safe."

Brooke waited for Hunter to laugh and say it was all a joke, but this kid was clearly delusional.

"I'm dead serious," he said.

"Yeah," Danny said, "Don't tell your mom neither, 'cause they'll get her too."

"She's not my mom." Brooke adjusted her hood to ward off the wind.

"Meet us tonight and we'll go somewhere safe," Hunter said.

"Where?"

"We don't *talk* about where we'll stay in case they're listening, or in case someone tells," Hunter said.

"You think I'm going to tattle on you?" Brooke let her mocking attitude ooze out.

"I hope you don't. We'll swing by your house tonight. Sneak out the—"

"Whoa." Brooke held up her hands. "I'm supposed to sneak out of my house at night, and what? Wander into the woods with you? Nice try, Romeo."

Brooke couldn't tell if Hunter was blushing or the cold air had pinched his cheeks for too long.

"It's not like that," he said.

A military police vehicle rolled slowly to the end of the cul-de-sac.

"Get down," Hunter whispered, ducking down with the small kids.

Brooke stood tall, making herself seen over the top of the playground hideaway.

The men were bundled in scarves and hats, covering their faces. From behind their black sunglasses, they peered out their windows toward Brooke. Karrie whimpered as she cowered down low. Some kind of darkness unsettled Brooke's nerves as they turned around in the cul-de-sac and headed back down the street.

These kids are really screwing with my head.

"We think they can't come out in daylight," little Danny said. "That's why they're all wrapped up."

"We've been here too long." Hunter stood once their vehicle was out of sight.

"Those MP's don't look like soul-sucking vampires to me," Brooke said. "They look *cold*."

"This isn't a joke," Hunter snapped.

The younger kids squeezed by Brooke and climbed down the ladder.

Brooke backed Hunter up against the blue plastic wall in the playground hideout. "Do you get some cheap thrill from scaring little kids?"

Hunter shook his head and answered, "I'm not the one scaring them."

She climbed down from the playground and Hunter followed.

With gentle eyes and a soft tone, he warned, "You don't have to meet us tonight, but please don't sleep at your house. Go somewhere else. We usually pick an empty house and take turns keeping watch."

"What about the kid in the house next door to me? She's fine. I saw her in the window earlier."

Hunter sighed. "We tried to get Ashley to come with us yesterday, but she wouldn't. They took Gavin and Max yesterday. Max's dad too. It's only a matter of time. They take a kid every night. Sometimes two."

Brooke backed away.

"And don't tell anyone," Hunter said. "Keep your mouth shut, or they'll get you and whoever you talk to."

After the sun had set, superstition got the best of Brooke and she began to wonder if there was any truth to Hunter's story. She turned the lights off in her room and sat in her bedroom window. The MP car drove through the neighborhood at least four times.

Mandy had already passed out in front of her portable DVD player.

Nervous energy coursed through Brooke. She didn't want to admit to herself that she was afraid, so she talked herself into going for a walk. She bundled up and stepped into the dark backyard and took a seat in a left-behind rusted lawn chair. Tucked within the pitch-black shadows, she looked to the stars.

Tires whispered on the pavement out front. A vehicle door clicked. She crept to the privacy fence and peeked through a knothole to see a black van parked in front.

No way.

A gloved hand reached around and muzzled Brooke's mouth. She thrashed, whipped around and threw a punch. Hunter ducked out of the way in time to miss her swing.

"Shhh!" He backed away with his hands up.

All three kids stood in the shadows dressed in black.

"They're here for you," Hunter said.

Brooke peeked through the knothole to see two figures in black tactical gear, rushing toward her front door. "Mandy," Brooke said.

"They're not there for her," Hunter said, tugging on her sleeve. "The young seem to be their priority."

"What do you mean—"

"Come on," Hunter said. The two little kids disappeared into the shadows of the tall trees behind her house. Hunter gestured for her to follow.

He led her through the woods with only a small amount of moonlight between the branches to guide their steps.

"Where are we going?" Brooke whispered.

"You just have to see it."

They hiked through the woods for several minutes, then sloshed through the wet leaves and rocks along a creek bed. It led to a drainage pipe that stood almost as tall as she did. It cut into the side of a hill.

Hunter hunched over and shuffled inside, looking back to Brooke. "Come on."

The younger kids waited behind her as she bent over and peeked into the blackness. An exit out the other side was visible. She stepped inside. The young kids followed until about half-way down the tunnel.

Hunter stopped them. "Wait here."

Without argument, the kids stayed put while Hunter and Brooke walked the last twenty yards to the other side. Out that end, there was a clearing in the trees. Weathered and broken targets dotted the overgrown field. Barely illuminated by the moon's glow, a narrow dirt road led to a large metal overhead door built into the side of a hill.

Clouds crept in from the west and threatened the last of their moonlight.

"They wanted you," Hunter whispered, "and because they didn't find you, they found someone else."

"Who—"

Brooke was silenced by the sound of a vehicle. The black van appeared without its headlights on.

"My friend Max had this theory that the young were more valuable souls in some way. They'll take adults, but they don't take them alive. They take them to shut them up. So nobody finds out about this place."

"That doesn't make sense. None of this makes sense," Brooke said.

The overhead door in the side of the hill hummed and cracked open, exposing a blinding light from inside. As the metal door rolled open, the younger kids whimpered down in the tunnel.

"They've seen this before," Hunter said.

A sound seeped out of the bright hole in the earth. At first it spilled out like a static, or some mechanical hum of a machine. But as Brooke listened in, it became clear.

Screams. Distant cries bled from the bunker. Countless horrific screams. The kind of screams like people were being tortured. The voices were so distant that Brooke couldn't discern if there were dozens or hundreds. Moaning, wailing, crying, and screeching sounds all blended together.

"The sound of souls being devoured," Hunter said. "That's what Max thought."

The black van pulled through the open door, disappearing into the light and swallowed by the screams. The door rolled shut.

A shiver sliced down Brooke's spine. Her pulse wailed between her ears and she backed away from the bars of the drainage pipe. "Who do they have?"

"There's only a few of us left," Hunter said. "Maybe Ashley? There was another new kid yesterday—maybe him."

"We have to tell someone," she said.

"There's nobody to tell," Hunter said, heading back down the tunnel. Karrie found Hunter in the darkness and hugged him around the waist.

"No signal," Brooke said. "No Wi-Fi."

"Exactly," Hunter said, exiting the tunnel into the creek bed. "It's getting colder. We should find a place for the night."

The vacant house across the street from Brooke's place became their hideout for the evening. They made it just before the snow started to fall so they didn't have to worry about covering their footprints. They broke in through the garage door, passing by shelves of tools that were left behind. The cabinets had some crackers and dry cereal to hold them over.

Hunter set up camp on the second floor where he could watch the street from the window. Danny and Karrie were bundled in a sleeping bag in the corner.

Brooke peered outside at her house across the street. "We have to get off this base," Brooke said.

"There's no leaving. Those guards with the wrapped faces grab kids who try to leave."

Brooke sighed. "Then we get a message out. Find a place that has a signal—"

"We've tried everything. There's no way to get a message off this base. It's not even a real base. It's like a gateway."

"A gateway to what?"

Hunter lit a small propane camp stove for warmth. "I don't know. But that place—The Underground—leads to something terrible."

"Are you saying it's a gateway to Hell?" Brooke asked.

"I don't believe in Hell."

"Then what is it?"

"I don't know!"

Brooke released a deep breath. "I'm getting off this base," she said. "I'll climb the perimeter fence if I have to."

"Barbed wire."

"Then we cut through the links! There are tools in the garage."

"We can't go anywhere!" Hunter said. "Don't you get it? They will stop you. They catch everyone that tries to leave. *Everyone*."

Karrie stirred in her sleeping bag.

Hunter quieted himself. "This is our end. If we run, it's over. If we *hide*, we live."

"That's no way to live," Brooke said. "I'm getting off this base. My dad will be back tomorrow."

Hunter laughed.

Brooke's gut turned sour. "He had to drop off Mandy and me and then take care of some … Why are you laughing?"

"Your dad is the one that dumped you off here. We're the rejects, Brooke. We're the kids of the good ol' tired retirees who didn't want to deal with us anymore. We've been *traded*."

Brooke's heart sank into the pit of her gut.

"That's what my friends and I figured out a few days ago. Our parents spent their lives struggling—and they'll continue to struggle even in retirement. My dad said the military screwed him out of his full retirement and disability pay."

"Parents wouldn't do that," Brooke said.

"You'd be surprised how many parents do. Dad never seemed like he enjoyed having a family."

"What are you saying?" Brooke covered her mouth, knowing exactly what Hunter was trying to get at. But she needed to hear it.

"Dad did an overnighter, then came home acting all weird. He was suddenly saying that the retirement thing worked out. He got a house in the mountains, wouldn't have to work another day in his life. That his years in combat would pay off after all. He would have a steady paycheck that he could live more than comfortably off of. But first, we had to do a short duty station here. Wherever *here* is. I don't even remember arriving. I was asleep."

The air in the room seemed to run out as Brooke realized she was asleep when she arrived at the base as well.

Hunter tucked his hands under his arms. "Our parents paid for their happily-ever-afters with *our* souls."

Brooke paced the room. "I've gotta get out of here."

"The snow is starting to stick," Hunter said. "That means footprints they can follow. Tonight, we stay low. We stay *here*."

Brooke ran downstairs to the garage and rummaged through the tools. She found a set of wire cutters.

I'm getting out of here.

The sound of vehicle tires pulled down the street. Brooke rushed upstairs to spy out the window.

"Be ready to run," Hunter said, shaking the younger kids awake. The black van parked in front of Brooke's house.

"They're trying to find me again," Brooke whispered.

Hunter nodded.

The men charged into Ashley's house.

Hunter sighed. "Damn it."

"What do we do?" Brooke asked.

"There's nothing we can do."

Across the street, two men left the house dragging a girl whose head was shrouded in a black bag.

"We have to help her!" Brooke said, turning to leave.

"It's too late." Hunter grabbed her arm. Brooke fought from his grip and ran out the front door. A layer of snow had already covered the ground. The men loaded Ashley into the van as Brooke charged out the front door.

"Hey!" It was the only word she could manage to get out.

They shut the van door and looked to Brooke. Their skin was no longer covered with scarves and sunglasses. Under the streetlamp's sodium glow, shriveled burned flesh scarred their faces. Where eyes and a nose should have been, there was nothing but red scar tissue. Black mouths hung wide open, unhinged and ready to devour like a snake.

Ashley thrashed inside the van, banging against the walls, as they climbed in.

Brooke leapt off the steps and raced down the road in a fury. Her feet slipped on the fresh-fallen snow as she screamed and chased after them. She followed until the van was out of sight, then gave up on her pursuit.

Forget Ashley. Make a run for it now.

She ran back to the house and ran upstairs. "Hunter!"

Brooke scrambled through every room, calling for them, but they were gone. Footsteps in the snow led from the back door, across the street and into the woods.

"Hunter!" She tried to track them down, but the snow had barely touched the ground beneath the canopy of trees. There were no footprints in the woods to follow. As she marched through the darkness, she whispered for Hunter, but nobody answered.

Screw this place.

Brooke maneuvered through the trees toward the perimeter of the base. She pushed through almost a quarter mile of brush and thorns, all the way to a narrow clearing at the chain link fence. It stood at least seven feet tall. Barbed wire ran along the top.

On the other side lay a marshy ditch with cattails leading up to an embankment. Beyond that, a highway. She knelt down in the snow and pulled the wire cutters from her pocket. Large snowflakes piled upon her head as she went to work cutting the first link. The relentless pounding of her pulse made her sick to her stomach. Hands trembled, but she kept cutting.

I can't believe Dad left me here.

But she could. She hadn't exactly been daughter-of-the-year.

A cracking branch from the woods froze her actions. She sat deadly still and slowly peeked over her shoulder at the darkness of the woods.

Go.

She went back to work, cutting one link at a time until she could pull away a small section to crawl through. Brooke looked over her shoulder one more time.

Nothing.

She lay down on her belly to shimmy underneath. The cold wet ground soaked through her sleeves as she wiggled her upper body through.

An exposed root lay just within reach. She stretched her fingers and wrapped them around it.

Almost.

Hands grabbed her ankles. Brooke shrieked as long fingers wrapped around her legs. Her screaming pierced the night air, echoing the screams that had poured out of The Underground earlier. Her heart pounded against the earth as she struggled to kick free. Brooke dug her fingers into the ground, raking the snow-dusted earth as something dragged her back under the fence and covered her head with a large black bag.

Under a shroud of darkness, all hope for escape disintegrated as the rattling sound of an overhead door opened. Ghostly cries surrounded her. The shrieks of the unwanted stung her ear drums as she sank deeper into the earth. Brooke, in one last defiant act against her father, refused to scream as her soul was stolen away to The Underground.

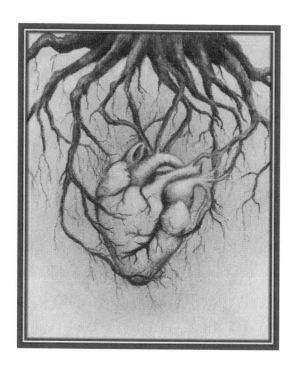

MALIGNANT ROOTS

KAREN'S CLENCHED FISTS went numb as she rode with her brother Derrick to their childhood home. She had no interest in visiting her father's grave. Mack Berrington had been a plague, spreading through the veins of everything he touched and turning it to rot and ruin. The kind of man, if given power, would have stretched his arms across the masses of humanity and sucked their life force until they were nothing but gnarled remnants of themselves.

It took years of distance from her father before Karen began to feel something like happiness. But somehow, he had always been there, haunting her, calling her back to feed on her despair. When he'd died, she swore she could feel it. Like a soft, sonic boom in the air around her—punching through her gut and filling her with hatred. Earth had finally rid itself of the terrible energy that pulsed beneath her father's fleshy exterior, and Karen couldn't help but feel relief.

Derrick pulled the car into the driveway. Cragged vines snaked up the once-white siding of the two-story farmhouse. The rosebushes lining the porch had dried into gray, snarled masses of thorny brush.

"Oh my God!" Derrick ran his fingers through his hair. "This place really fell apart over the last year. It was all good when we buried him."

"You mean when you *planted* him?"

Mack's ashes had been placed in the root ball of a young elm tree and buried in the middle of the backyard. Karen had refused to attend the funeral, but Derrick finally guilted her into visiting.

When she stepped outside the car, a magnetic-like repulsion warned her not to go any farther—to get back in the car and never go near the place again.

"Come on, Karen."

"I'm not going in the house." *Too many bad memories. Mom strangled near-to-death. Derrick under the bed while I was being slammed against the wall. Evening after evening of being frozen in fear until I grew into a resentful and spiteful woman, incapable of trust.*

Her father was a poison, and now even in death, his memory poisoned the house into disrepair.

"Okay, we don't have to go inside," Derrick said. "We'll just go out back, pay our respects, and leave."

"I have no respect to pay."

Derrick sighed, closed the car door, and went ahead without her around the side of the house.

Karen folded her arms tight against her body. *He's here. That bastard. I can feel him.*

"Karen!" Derrick called from out back.

With great trepidation, she followed. Dried, yellow grass crunched beneath her feet. Everything was dead—the grass, the hedgerows under the kitchen windows. As she rounded the corner of the house, she spotted Derrick, frozen mid-step.

No, that's not Derrick. Just a dried up old tree trunk.

Karen approached the gray-brown tree. Thick, fresh vines—more like roots—snaked up its base. Two limbs stretched out like arms. Her blood chilled as she leaned in to get a closer look. Etched within the bark was the striking resemblance of a face. His mouth agape, eye sockets empty. The shape of a man, solidified into a decrepit lifeless tree.

Derrick?

Her breath hitched as she followed his gaze to a massive elm tree—old, sturdy, and standing almost as tall as the house. It dominated the back lot. The only thing there that was alive. Twisted, gnarled branches reached outward and over her head. Great roots had pushed up portions of the lawn all the way to the house. One had forced itself through a window; shards of glass lay beneath. The great elm's root structure had invaded the walls, choking the life out of her childhood home—not that there was ever any life in it.

Nailed into the bark of the elm was a simple name plaque: Mack Berrington. *Impossible.* The young sapling containing the ashes of her father had grown fifty years in the span of one.

The ground pulsed beneath Karen's feet. A slow, intoxicated *blub-blub* that crept up her legs and into her veins. A warm breeze rustled the leaves in Mack's branches, brushed her hair away from her face, and kissed at her neck.

It's him. Dad, what did you do?

Tears welled in her eyes as she fawned over her brother's petrified form. His limbs dried and crumbled under her gentle touch. All life and energy had been vacuumed out by the massive elm.

Trembling, Karen backed away.

Roots birthed from the soil, shaking the earth beneath her feet. The roots around Derrick slithered up and through his trunk, then sprouted from his mouth and eyes.

The elm's hefty boughs swelled and creaked as Karen scrambled to get away. A thick limb, stretching out toward the horizon—the kind a tire swing could be hung from if ever such a happy family could enjoy it—lowered to stop her.

The soil-encrusted roots from below snaked up her calves. They constricted her thighs and belly.

Her arms drained of color. Skin crusted and flaked as the rot metastasized. She hardened on the inside, not from fear or resilience like in the past, but from the scar-like tissue spreading from cell to cell.

Please, Dad. Don't...

Her father advanced his diseased roots through her body and pulled every last bit of energy from her until she fossilized in place beneath his branches.

Mack Berrington sucked the life out of everything he touched.

HELPING HANDS RETREAT

SARAH CREPT DOWN an old pockmarked road with a watchful eye on her rearview mirror. Dust clouds lifted from asphalt and swirled in the red glow of tail lights as she headed to the retreat.

A *retreat* they called it. Anything would be a retreat compared to the life she had been living. She'd rather be lost on this desolate stretch of unmarked road than to turn the car around and risk facing Wade. She choked on the thought of his name. The thought that he could be a mile behind her, tracking her like a coonhound after the fox. There was no turning back now.

Trees and thick shrubbery lined the ever-narrowing road. Sarah wasn't sure if she made the correct turn half an hour ago when she came to the forked road. She had been certain she was heading the right way until now. Deep ditches on each side made it too difficult to turn around.

Headlight beams exposed a chain link fence ahead. Its open gate swayed and creaked in the breeze. She rolled to a stop at the entrance. On the road's edge, an aged plank sign painted with white block letters read: *Helping Hands Recovery Retreat.*

She could have sworn it was called *Hands of Hope Retreat.* The brochure she had found at the women's clinic promised shelter for abused women. The trifold never left the office with her. Bringing it home for Wade to find was far too risky, so she took mental note of the address. Perhaps her memory of the name was wrong.

It wasn't the beautifully landscaped guarded iron-gates she had imagined. To verify that she was in the right place, she turned on the location to the car's GPS. It had been off all day. Knowing Wade, he'd find a way to track her down if she left it on.

Ahead, small dots of yellow light marked the presence of buildings. She released the breath she had been holding all day and drove through the gate. The dense woods ended and the drive. An open field stretched well beyond the moonlight's reach. The road turned to gravel and crunched beneath her tires. She glanced in the rearview mirror again as if Wade would hear the crushing rocks all the way from back home and come after her. She took his car, after all. She should've slashed the tires of his pick-up to give herself a better head start.

The GPS map wouldn't load. *Come on.*

Each crunch and clack of the gravel made her flinch. Her fists clenched the steering wheel like it were the reins to a horse. If she held tight enough and closed her eyes, she could trust her horse to take her where she needed to be.

It worked when she was sixteen. Mom and Dad had been fighting again, so she climbed onto Midnight with no other plan but to get away. She had ridden for hours, down to the river bank and all the way to the next town. Freedom in her hair, she closed her eyes and let Midnight guide her to a place where nobody screamed at each other. Where nobody stormed into her room to take their anger out on her. That taste of escape had lasted until sunset that day. Then she headed back home because there was nowhere else to go. Her parents hadn't even noticed she was gone.

She wished Wade were the type to not notice, but she knew better than to think he wouldn't find her. He always knew where she was.

The rhythmic clopping of hooves approached from behind. Sarah pressed on the brake to listen. Had she imagined the sound of the horse? In the glow of her tail lights, a person sat on horseback. Her heart stopped as a man with a large build—a build like Wade's—climbed off his steed. She sensed an icy glare. It cut through the glass of the back window, prying for answers about what business she had being there.

Don't be ridiculous. If it were Wade, he would've already been dragging her out of the car.

She continued down the gravel road toward the lit structures, leaving the man on the horse behind her. Though intimidating, he brought Sarah a bit of hope for what was to come. Horseback riding was featured in the brochure as an activity for the guests at the shelter. *Guests*, they were referred to. Guests with horrible nightmarish pasts, smiling, padding their kayaks and riding their horses, as if the world had never harmed them.

Five rustic structures stood like toothpick homes, nothing like the depicted elaborate cabins with rock facades. A stout woman in a purple winter coat waddled out of one of the houses and approached the car. Sarah rolled down the window.

"Welcome to the Helping Hands Retreat, dear." An icy fog spilled from her mouth carrying the scent of peppermint.

"I'm not sure if I found the right place."

"I'm sure you have." A wide smile showcased her snow white teeth.

"I saw a brochure last week, but this doesn't quite look—"

"You need help," the round-faced woman said. "A chance to get back on your feet. To start over, right?"

"Something like that…" Sarah waited for the woman's angle. Any moment, she'd ask her for money, or shove a Bible in her lap.

"That's what we do, dear. We help people who need a clean start. You're in the right place. Come."

The premises were not as upscale as expected, but Sarah didn't care. Anything was better than lying in that bed beside Wade. Anything was better than living in fear.

"Our parking lot is down the hill, behind the barn. But it's not a path you want to walk at night. Just leave your car here. We'll take care of it in the morning."

She cut the engine and stepped out. The cold air bit at her bruised arms before she pulled her hoodie from the car and slipped it on.

The woman's eyes seemed to track Sarah's discomfort. "You've missed dinner. But we can get you settled in a private room." She interlaced her white-gloved fingers—the kind of formal gloves that are typically reserved for special occasions.

"That would be wonderful."

"I'm Mary." Her fierce and prying eyes didn't match her warm smile.

Sarah followed her to an unusually long rectangular house. White latticework enclosed the crawlspace below. At the end of the house, three steps led to a door. Inside, a hallway stretched the length of the house. Rooms lining each side like a hotel. A shared bathroom and a common room sat at the end.

At eight o'clock, Mary left Sarah in room number four. All of the guests had retired to their rooms for the evening already, so she wouldn't meet anyone until morning. *Strange.*

Her drafty ten by ten room lacked the shabby chic décor of the brochure's pictures. A twin bed with a two-inch thick mattress sat pressed into the corner. A nightstand held a welcome basket of toiletries. A towel, toothbrush, petroleum jelly, a set of hat and gloves—like a care package for a homeless person. She had no belongings with her. Other than the little bit of cash pulled from the account Wade allowed her access to, Sarah brought nothing. Not even her phone. Knowing Wade, he'd report his car as stolen, but surely a women's shelter would protect her against such allegations considering she was running for her life.

The soft blue glow of moonlight seeped in from behind the curtain of her private room, exposing shadowy lines—bars on the windows. She grasped the cold iron bars. Bitter air drafted from between the gaps in the floorboards and nipped at her bare feet. Outside, a large open field sprawled beneath the moonlight.

She dreamed about her potential new life. Right out there where the field meets the trees—that's where she'd ride. The dream faded as an icy chill crawled up her spine. Someone was there. Eyes watching her. She tried to shrug it off as paranoia, but it persisted. It hung eerily in the air like pressure before a storm.

Thin walls muffled the gentle sobs of a woman next door in room number three.

She shut the curtains and tiptoed barefoot across the creaking wooden floors. In the center of the room she froze. No draft seeped through the floor here. A gentle bulge of the floorboard pushed against her foot. Something was under the house. Sarah gasped and jumped to her bed. The wood clunked as whatever was under there moved. It crawled in the dirt below and moved toward the edge of the house.

She leapt from the safety of her bed toward the window and threw open the curtains. A shadow of a person drew out of view around the side of the house.

Her heart throbbed in her ears. The will to scream, to call for help, clotted in her throat.

The sobs of the woman next door ceased.

Sarah craned her neck to see around the corner of the house out the window, but the intruder was gone. As she pulled away and crossed her arms over her chest, she managed to speak. "Did anyone see that?" Her voice too meek for anyone to hear.

Outside, a deep throaty voice cried out, "No!"

Sarah covered her mouth. Eyes wide open, she cocked her head with her ear pressed between the bars of the window.

A faint growling screech. "I'm sorry." The words faded into guttural sounds of agony.

Sarah scrambled to get her shoes on and left her room. Shaking, she crept down the empty hallway to the exit. The knob wouldn't turn.

"Hello?" she said, voice quaking as it echoed off the barren hallway walls.

The doorknob defied her. She cranked harder.

Locked from the outside. *Trapped.* Sarah backed away from the door. Screaming outside persisted so she ran back to the only place she could—room number four. She locked herself in and climbed onto the bed. Knees held tight to her chest. Soft whimpers bled through the walls next door and into her soul. Curled up against the wall, Sarah froze. A familiar feeling she'd get before Wade would go into a rampage. Her vision would tunnel and she'd stiffen as she awaited his rage. They say fight or flight are the two options, but nobody talks about *fright.* Like a damn opossum playing dead. That state of remaining so perfectly still that, maybe, if she didn't fight or run, she'd stand a chance of surviving after all. So Sarah sat there, eyes wide and quiet, breaths controlled and still, being as invisible as she could manage until everything blew over. For Sarah, *fright* always won.

Sarah barely slept all night. Up before sunrise while the house was dead still, she cleaned up in the communal bathroom and waited to confront Mary.

"Coyote," she said when Sarah asked Mary about the intruder under the house.

"It was too big to be a coyote," Sarah said. "It was a person and … Is everyone okay? I heard someone screaming last night."

"Honey." She leaned in closer. "I'm not gonna lie. The people that come here have problems. They got demons to work out, and sometimes those demons get the best of them. I'm sure you noticed the bars on the windows. We have to keep people safe."

"The bars are to keep people *in*? I thought they were to protect us from outsiders."

"Outsiders are rarely the problem." Mary leaned in to whisper. "The problem lies inside of ourselves."

"So this is a place for dangerous people?" Sarah watched as those people passed by her room to exit the house. Most kept their heads down and didn't look, but one gray-haired woman peeked from under her silvery strands.

Mary continued. "Everyone who's here has got their sins they gotta atone for."

"I'm not here because I sinned."

"You don't sin?" Mary smiled.

"I'm here because I'm escaping an abusive relationship. I thought that's what this place was."

"I see." Mary shifted her weight and tilted her head. "You poor dear."

"The road forked a few miles off the interstate. I thought I was heading toward a place called Hands of Hope, but ended up here. It's clear now that I'm at the wrong place."

"But you're not, dear. You see...you escaped a horrible man, didn't you? But to do that, what did you have to do? You cleaned out the bank account? Took his car?"

"But there was no other way. How did you know—"

"It's my job to know. Come now." Mary guided Sarah outside into the cold dry air. Her tiny white-gloved hand pressed between Sarah's shoulder blades to direct her to the next building.

"Where's my car?" Sarah asked, crossing her bare arms to keep warm.

"Well that wasn't *your* car, was it?" Mary smiled. "It was Wade's car."

Sarah's blood chilled at the sound of his name. "How do you know his name?"

"It was on the registration."

"You went through the glove box?"

"Well now." She waved her hand as if shooing a fly. "We can't be too careful. Come eat some breakfast, then we'll talk about getting you on your way. What kind of Christian would I be if I let you go all the way back down that road, and then up into the mountains on an empty stomach?"

An inadequate wood stove sat in the corner. Five guests were already seated, eating at two of the round tables. They wore winter hats and mittens—they needed them in this drafty building. Sarah couldn't believe the facilities at a place like this were so terrible. They needed to be reported to someone. The guests all wore the same shirt, a black and red flannel. They spooned scrambled eggs into their mouths without exchanging words.

Sarah approached the breakfast bar with Mary on her heels. A gray-haired woman, frail and trembling, stood behind the counter. Her hands, covered with green rubber gloves, shook as she scooped a meager pile of eggs and hash browns onto her plate.

"This is Eleanor. She works in the cafeteria this week. It's all part of it," Mary said. "We all do our part to be helpful in our community. *Everyone* has a job. Helping hands—"

"—are clean hands," Eleanor said with her head down.

"Thank you." Sarah turned away from the counter and sat at a table with three others.

A man with greasy black hair poking out from under his hat, sat at the table.

"Have a seat here with Jacob," Mary said.

Jacob's unkempt beard held crumbs of yellow egg. His gaze broke from his rubbery pile of eggs when Sarah sat to join him. He rocked in his seat, hands tucked under the table.

Sarah rubbed her cold fingers together and warmed them with her breath. "It's so cold in here."

Jacob gasped. "Sh-sh-she didn't wash her hands!" He backed away from the table and pointed to her. "She didn't wash her hands!"

"I washed them," Sarah said.

"Jacob." Mary said, approaching his side.

"It's not fair!" Spit strung between his lips. He rocked, keeping his arms crossed in front of his body.

The other guests remained quiet, but eyes were locked on Sarah.

"Jacob!" Mary's voice cracked as she yelled.

He sat down and quieted himself.

Mary folded her hands together. Her crisp white gloves pressed against her chin. "Don't worry about her, Jacob. She'll wash like everyone else." She stood taller and looked around the room. "Because helping hands—"

"—are clean hands." All the guests said it in unison.

After breakfast, Sarah went to the bathroom in the barracks house and as she headed toward the exit, Mary entered. In one arm, she carried a black and red flannel. She extended a hand, gesturing for Sarah to go into room number four.

Sarah stopped at the doorway.

Mary extended a folded flannel shirt and a pair of canvas gloves.

"What's this?"

"Your work clothes," Mary said, stepping forward to force Sarah into room number four.

Sarah stepped back, but then held her stance in the doorway. "I'm sorry. I appreciate you letting me stay here, but I have to go. I'd like to get my car now."

"Wade's car." Mary's friendly demeanor diminished.

"I was heading to the women's retreat. You have to understand. I wasn't supposed to come here."

"But you did." Her words cracked like a whip on the cold air. "And everyone that comes here, comes for a reason. You were sent to atone for your sins."

"Please," she said, voice trembling. "I want to go."

"Tom!" Mary blocked the door frame so Sarah couldn't leave.

Eleanor passed by, looking up long enough to warn Sarah with a shake of her head. Her large round eyes were backlit with a sense of urgency.

A man well over six feet tall stormed down the hallway and filled the doorway.

"My dear," Mary said. "You can leave once you pay off your debt for staying last night."

"I have money," Sarah said. "I can pay—"

"You have stolen money, you thief!" Mary's sugar sweet voice dissolved into a snarl.

Tom took a step into her room. His chiseled face, scarred and deformed, scowled beneath a thick red beard.

"When your work is done, when your sins are atoned for, that's when you leave."

"How long does that take?"

"As long as people need." Mary gritted her teeth and then took a deep breath. "Come, dear. You don't want to make this difficult."

Sarah took the flannel and gloves from Mary and closed her door behind them after they left.

Outside, Sarah met up with the others, who were already working on tilling the ground along the gravel road. Tom sat on a brown and white painted horse near the entrance. A shotgun hung over his shoulder. He heeled the horse and galloped up to Sarah. Dust kicked up as he stopped beside her. He put a hand on his gun and eyed Sarah as if reminding her to do as she's told.

Mary put a hand on Sarah's shoulder. "Let's be a good girl."

A good girl. Sarah retracted into that state of survival—of doing what she was told. Doing what was expected. Wade used to say it. *Be a good girl, and I won't get mad.* As if she were a dog threatened by her master with beatings if she didn't obey his command to heel.

Sarah kept her head down, pulling weeds and tilling the dry winter-blistered earth with the others for hours. It was still better than living with Wade. These thoughts disgusted her.

Her nose and her fingers numbed, so Sarah removed her work gloves and rubbed her hands together. Warm, moist air brought back some sensation.

She seemed to catch Eleanor's attention but when Sarah looked at her, she looked away.

Eleanor's hands shook as she worked the ground with her handheld tiller. Her fingers wouldn't grasp the handle completely.

"Are your hands okay," Sarah whispered.

"Shh." Eleanor wouldn't look up.

"Are they numb? Do you need another pair of gloves?"

"Shh!" Eleanor's nostrils flared and a tear streaked down her cheek.

Mary worked ten yards away at the tilled ground around the lattice. She had exchanged her fancy white gloves, for purple gardening gloves. She buried tulip bulbs, carefully situating each one. Jacob with the greasy black hair, gave up on his tools and used the tips of his toes to dig away at the ground. He tucked his hands under his arms. All of these people would end up with frostbite if they didn't get to warm up soon.

Breaking the deadly silence, Mary stood up and pointed toward the tree line at a coyote. "Tom!"

Tom nudged the horse with his heel and trotted off the gravel road, away from the open gate. He aimed the shotgun at the coyote in the distance. Before firing, he lowered the gun and edged closer. He aimed again.

Jacob shifted twitchy eyes from the direction of the coyote to Mary. He took off in a sprint. Dust kicked up behind his boots as he headed along the dried grass toward the gate.

With Tom and Mary's attention on the coyote, maybe Jacob had a chance. All the guests stopped working and stared.

Their gazes pierced the air. Sarah's silent screams cheered him on. It seemed like a good idea—to run. But there was nowhere to run to, not with Tom on that horse. Maybe he could make it down to the barn where the parking lot was. Maybe this guy would go for a car. Would he have the keys? Maybe Sarah should have run too.

Jacob made it through the open gate. Mary and Tom were still distracted by the coyote.

The shot gun fired, blasting up a chunk of dirt at the coyote's feet.

"Damn!" Tom followed the coyote with the end of the shotgun.

"Tom!" Mary pointed toward the gate as Jacob escaped.

Tom spun his horse around and kicked his heel into its side to take off.

"Come on folks," Mary said. "I think that's enough of that for today. Let's go back to your rooms to warm up." She gestured for them to follow her as Tom galloped out of sight.

Sarah got in line with everyone else and walked back to her room. As she closed her door, a gunshot in the distance made her freeze mid-step. Her feet pressed hard into the floor, like gravity could yank her through the wooden planks. She would have liked to let it pull her right down into the ground, buried away where nobody could find her.

Sarah knelt to inspect the wood floor and the cracks between. The old boards bowed under her weight. Rusty nails eroding in their holes. She pried on a board where it appeared to be weakest. The edge lifted.

Fingers would not fit between the spaces to get enough torque on it, so Sarah dug into her welcome basket of supplies. The toothbrush could be used for leverage. She wedged the board upward, and the nail came with it, wiggling out of place with little effort. She got to work on the second board—three would be enough for her frame to squeeze through. The boards came loose and she stuck her head into the space beneath the house.

Instinct told her to run—to get out now, but she had to be smarter. Tom was still out there. She placed the boards back into position and waited on her bed as the daylight lingered. There was a knock at her door.

"Yes?" Sarah took a deep breath and was ready to play it casual. No different than the hours before she had left Wade.

Mary opened her door and Sarah stood to greet her.

"What a day, huh?" Mary smiled and stepped one foot inside her door. "I want you to know that Jacob is alright now. Tom caught up with him and he's resting in his room."

"I thought I heard—"

"The gunshot, right?" Mary nodded. "That coyote. There've been reports of rabies. Tom saw it stalking Jacob, so he put it down. He could have been seriously hurt out there."

Lies. "Mary, may I ask…"

Mary unclasped her white-gloved fingers and spread her arms apart as if she were an open book.

"Why wasn't he allowed to leave?"

"Jacob is a violent man. We can't let people wander off while they are in our care."

"So, what about me?"

Mary took a step back and folded her hands back together. "You?"

"I'm not violent. I'm not a danger. I've done the work you've asked of me."

"But you're not perfect yet." Mary's voice lowered and her face dropped with an earnest message. "Everyone thinks they don't sin."

"I don't think that," Sarah argued, "but I don't deserve to be imprisoned."

"You don't deserve..." she laughed. "It's not about what you deserve. It's about cleansing our hands of our sins and becoming a better community in the process, because helping hands..." Mary's mouth stretched into a slim smile.

Sarah hesitated, but did as expected. "Are clean hands?"

"Good girl, dear. Dinner is at six thirty. Tom and I will stop by for hand-washing just before that."

"Hand-washing?"

"Hush now. It's been a long day." Mary left.

The sun set and Sarah sat against the wall on her bed, waiting for the sky to darken. Waiting for nightfall to cloak her escape.

"Don't worry," a voice made its way through the wall from room number three. It was Eleanor.

Sarah got to her knees, palms and ear to the wall to listen.

"It hurts bad the first time, but you get used to it," Eleanor said.

"What?"

"Hand-washing. It hurts. My hands still hurt. Just don't run and don't fight," she said.

Don't run. Don't fight.

"He watches us from under the house." Eleanor's nervous hitching breath could be heard through the wall. "Tom comes after dinner and tries to watch us undress. When he gets caught, he gets in trouble and pays for it."

While Eleanor talked, Sarah knelt down to remove the loose planks from the floor. Twilight settled in and the moon rose above the tree line. Heavy feet clomped on the stairs out front and Sarah lowered her body into the crawlspace. She returned the planks to their position and crawled toward the loose panel of lattice. Mary stalled at the edge of the house as Tom and Mary approached.

Tom carried a five-gallon bucket. He opened the door for Mary and they both entered.

Sarah crawled out from under the house and crouched down in shadow. Light from room number one drew her closer. The curtains were shut, save for a small gap that allowed a strip of light to spill onto the ground.

Curiosity drew Sarah closer. Inside, Tom stood over a frail man with drooping eyes. He sat on the bed with Mary by his side. She rubbed his back while he sobbed and held out his hands.

Mary pulled each glove from his fingers, exposing pink and shriveled flesh. Burns over the entire surface of his hands from wrist to fingertip. He trembled as Tom held his forearms and Mary placed a cloth in his mouth.

Tom forced the man's hands into the bucket. The liquid inside bubbled and spit while the man screamed through the cloth between his teeth. The chemical in the bucket splattered onto the floor, hissing.

Sarah covered her mouth to shield a gasp and backed away from the window. She needed to save him, to stop this. For a moment, she thought she could muster the courage for a heroic rescue—rushing inside and fighting them off, or perhaps she could find Tom's gun and...

Before she could finish the thought, she sprinted across the moonlit field toward the entrance gate. Wide open. She didn't know which direction the car lot was in, or where the keys to the car would be, so she ran the only direction she was sure of.

As she neared the gate, the sound of a whinny startled her and she dropped to the ground anticipating Tom to take a shot at her. Bits of gravel pressed into her hands and knees. When she opened her eyes in the darkness, there was Tom's painted horse standing before her. But Tom was nowhere in sight.

Screams echoed from the houses and split the night. Sarah untied the horse from the fence and climbed on. *I'll get help.*

The cold air sliced through her lungs as she cut down the old road. It was a long way back to the fork, at least half an hour by car.

Get help—she chanted under her breath.

In the distance, a set of headlights approached. *Thank God!*

But the short-lived beacon of hope unraveled into a new nightmare as Sarah considered who it could be. What if they were connected to Helping Hands in some way? What if she were to be dragged back to that place?

She had to get out of sight. Sarah climbed off the horse and rushed him off the road, down into the ditch into the blackness of the trees' shadows.

A pickup truck blasted by, blaring music. It looked a lot like Wade's truck but it was too dark and too fast to tell.

Her heartbeat thrummed in her temples as she led the horse back onto the road. Sarah pressed forward. She wanted to close her eyes and let the horse take her away, but her fate was in her own hands now.

Sarah stayed alert. On the road for over an hour, down to the fork, then cutting up the mountain road she should have taken the day before. The cold wind lashed through her hair as she made her escape.

The landscape turned from moonlit wild brush to pruned bushes and mulch-circled trees. Spot lights lit up a fountain and a stone sign read *Hands of Hope Retreat*.

THE MAN IN THE PICKUP truck left his music blasting as he pulled through the gate of Helping Hands Retreat.

A small round woman shuffled out of the house toward his vehicle. A burly guy stood in the doorway, holding a five-gallon bucket as moaning poured from the building.

"What the hell?"

"Welcome!" she said.

"I'm looking for my wife." Wade said. "Bitch stole my car. I tracked the GPS here."

"You must mean Sarah." The woman smiled. "She's inside. We've been taking good care of her."

"Well she don't need to be taken care of." Wade got out of the truck and put his hands in his pockets to keep warm.

"Would you like to see her?" she asked.

"What the hell do you think?"

Mary guided him toward the house.

"She's in her room. Come. You're just in time for dinner. Let's wash your hands."

SEVERED CONNECTION

IF CHARLOTTE COULDN'T TALK to Devon, or feel his touch ever again, she just might choke to death on the huge pile of ash filling her insides. She missed her husband so much it felt like little pieces of her innards burned away. But the ash had nowhere to go, it just kept piling up in her gut, into a huge mountain of gray sadness that reached all the way up to her throat. If only she could make it all blow away. That's why she came to this place. To find a way to talk to her Devon again.

But she screwed up. She never should have come to this man's house for help. Her late husband had warned her about this guy, but it's not like she had a lot of options. What was she supposed to do with the suffocating feeling of loneliness? Nothing?

No. Charlotte wouldn't let that happen. Devon had always said, "Go get what you want, girl." And she intended to.

Ty, a thirty-something man with a YouTube channel on communicating with the dead, sat in a musty recliner across from her. Skin so pasty, it looked like he was battered in flour, but never deep fried. Charlotte didn't like to make first-impression judgments, but his greasy appearance made it difficult. A pair of wire-rimmed glasses held for dear life to his plump face. His eyes must've had breast magnets in them because they were stuck all over hers. And leg magnets, too. The jerk couldn't keep his gaze above her neck.

You better not try to make a move on me. Charlotte quelled the rising vomit in her throat.

Years ago, Devon served with Ty during a disaster relief mission to Haiti. After that deployment, Ty got involved in the supernatural world—ghost hunting and witchcraft and all sorts of weird shit. When Devon found out that Ty had moved to New Orleans, just a few miles from their neighborhood, he warned Charlotte about him. Like a parent would finger the neighborhood sexual predator, Devon pulled up a map and pointed out the house that Charlotte should avoid at all costs.

"He's a pervert, disgusting. You don't want to know the things he got away with, babe," Devon had said. "Someone should've cut that guy's dick off years ago... for the sake of humanity."

Ty licked his lips while his eyes scanned from the floor at her red heels, up to her knees, her breasts...

Charlotte squeezed her knees together so hard the bones rubbed. With a feigned smile she asked, "So can you help me?"

Ty stood up from the creaky brown recliner.

Nervous energy coursed through her. A discreet slip of her hand dug into the purse at her hip. Concealed in the casing of a standard ballpoint pen, was a razor-sharp blade. She brought it with her everywhere, but today was the first time she'd ever considered using it. She had practiced popping the cap off and stabbing a would-be threat before. The easily-manipulated cap twisted in her fingers. All she had to do is pop it off and slice into this pervert if he tried anything.

Ty shuffled around the coffee table full of empty soda cans and Dorito crumbs. His boxy frame blocked out the sunlight seeping through the almost-closed curtains. Pale fingers with unkempt nails ran along the wall of shelves hanging over the mantle as he edged closer to the couch. The shelves held jars with pink fluid and body parts—a tiny heart, a paw. A coiled snake. Also adorning the shelves were old books, dusty ceramic bowls, beads, and Barbie dolls of all things.

"Considering I knew Devon personally," Ty said, "it should be easy to communicate with him."

"Really?" Charlotte's heart fluttered. Eyes watered at the prospect of speaking with her one true love again.

"Sure." Ty sat beside her.

A plume of dust particles exploded into the column of sunlight. His weight forced her to sink into the cushion closer to him. She scooted over to put some space between them, but Ty leaned back and stretched his arm out on the back of the couch behind her, like a bad date in a movie theater.

Sweat slicked her grip on the pen-knife, still tucked in her purse between her and Ty. Ready to stab him in the thigh if he tried anything… *Maybe I should go for the throat.* But that was way too bloody and violent. *No.* A quick jab to the thigh and she could make a run for it. *Don't even try it, asshole.*

Ty let out a roaring yawn.

"So what do we do?" she asked, adding another couple inches between them. "Ouija board?"

He winked. "You know your stuff." A cloud of corn-chip halitosis spilled from his mouth. He scratched his dark hair. It could've been brown, or maybe grease-drenched ashy blonde. Steel blue eyes met with hers as he leaned closer. A hand brushed her shoulder.

Charlotte sprung up from the couch, but her hair snagged. She fell back into her seat with a grunt.

"Woops!" Ty said.

Charlotte slid her thumb into position to pop the cap off the pen, ready to thrust it into the man's thigh.

"Sorry! My watch is caught in your hair." Ty kept his arm stretched out, keeping his body a respectful distance away. "Oh my God. I'm so sorry. Hold still and I'll try to get it unstuck."

With his wristwatch snagged in her curly black hair, Ty reached with his other hand across the coffee table, knocking cans onto the floor to grab a pair of scissors. "May I?"

"Just do it," Charlotte said through clenched teeth.

"Got it!" Ty stood up, flashed his silver watch with a nervous shake and slipped it in the pocket of his faded gray hoodie. "I'm so sorry."

Charlotte adjusted her hair, inspecting the shorter curl with her fingers. "I'm not comfortable being touched."

"I'm sorry."

If he said "sorry" one more time, she might have to stab him after all.

"I didn't mean to. I was just pulling my arm back and it got snagged. All those curls." His palms were up in defense and she almost believed the clumsy idiot. "Anyway. Let me get set up and we'll get started."

"Wait," Charlotte said. "What's this going to cost?"

Ty shrugged. "I dunno. Hundred bucks?"

"A hundred bucks?! What if it doesn't work?"

"It'll work. Guaranteed."

"How will I know you're not scamming me?"

"I wouldn't scam *you*."

"I don't know. I might need time to think about this." Charlotte was too smart to give money to this guy. But desperation motivated her to ignore those reservations for the slim chance that it could work.

"You can think about it," Ty said. "But I can't promise I'll be available tomorrow. Or the next day. In fact, I'm in the middle with optioning my show to Netflix." He arched his eyebrows. "So, I might not be available for months, actually."

Bullshit. But Charlotte didn't care.

124

"You wanna wait that long?" Ty shrugged. "Doesn't matter to me."

Charlotte rolled her eyes, released the pen-knife, and dipped into her purse for the cash.

After clearing the coffee table, Ty lit some candles and set a wooden Ouija board in front of Charlotte. He shut the gap in the curtains, bringing darkness to the dank one-bedroom home. The room flickered in an orange glow of candlelight while Ty knelt on the opposite side of the table.

"You'll need to be comfortable. Would you like to borrow some sweats?" Ty interlocked his fingers, squirming.

Vomit tried to creep up Charlotte's throat. "No. I'm fine."

"Constricting clothing can impede the flow of our energies..." Ty swayed side to side, stretching out his arms like a wave. "...making it harder for spirits to make contact."

"I'm not wearing your clothes." Charlotte furrowed her brow. She should've left a long time ago, but she was so close to what she wanted.

"No," Ty laughed. "Not *my* clothes. I have a change of clothes here just for clients."

Eww. How is that less creepy?

"I'm fine." Charlotte slid out of her fitted leopard-print jacket and slung it over the arm of the couch, just in case he wasn't completely full of shit.

"That should help." Ty locked eyes on her tank top.

They placed their fingers on the wooden planchette.

125

"I see you know where to put your fingers. Very good," Ty said.

"Don't patronize me. Of course I know what to do. I watch TV."

Ty put his hands up in surrender. "I'm just saying you have good form. Like a natural."

Charlotte scowled and shook her head.

Returning his fingers to the planchette, Ty rolled his neck. "Meditating, deep breaths. Relax. Think about him," he said, locked on her gaze instead of her breasts, for once.

Charlotte pictured Devon's face. That smile that made her knees quake. That silly mustache he grew on deployment. She hated that lip caterpillar and he knew it. Devon shaved it, but now whenever she pictured him, she couldn't help but see that goofy stache. An almost-smile worked its way to the corners of her mouth. The crinkles around his eyes. Black hair, always like he stepped fresh out of the barber shop. His smooth skin and soft lips on her neck. God, she missed him. Stinging tears threatened to escape. She closed her eyes.

"Devon?" Ty said. "Are you here?"

The planchette shifted left.

Charlotte pulled her hands away with a gasp. "Did you move that?"

A sly smile crossed Ty's thin lips. Scruffy black prickles of facial hair seemed to wiggle on his jaw in the flickering candlelight. "I don't fake the Ouija. You don't mess with this stuff. We're making contact. Put your fingers back on the thing."

Charlotte did as instructed.

"Devon, is that you?" Ty let out a short gasp. "I feel him in the room."

Charlotte's heart sped despite her reluctance to believe him.

"He's here. Do you feel that, Charlotte?" Ty shuddered. His eyes met with hers—they were bright, excited, and for once she began to believe him.

Nothing. Charlotte closed her eyes and put more energy into her thoughts about Devon.

"Devon?" Charlotte whispered.

The planchette shifted again. This time, she kept her hands in place and the damned thing slid like butter all the way across the board to *YES.*

A quick burst of joy exploded from within. For the first time in months, Charlotte let out a laugh. Tears broke away from her eyelids and rolled down her cheek.

"I miss you, Baby," she said.

Too smooth to be controlled by the clumsy moron sitting across from her, the planchette glided across the board one letter at a time spelling out: *I love you.*

"Charlotte," Ty said. "Ask him anything you want."

"Are you okay?" She wiped her wet cheeks with her bare shoulder. A chill raised her arm hairs to attention. "Please be okay," she whispered. "Please be happy."

Yes.

Skepticism melted away. The planchette moved without prompting, spelling out another word. *Sexy.*

"Oh," Ty said, blushing. "Awkward."

Charlotte laughed. *Typical Devon.* How she longed to hold him again. "I wish I could hug you."

...You can.

Ty took his fingers away from the board and scratched behind his ear. Using the corner of this gray hoodie, he wiped the lenses of his wire-rimmed glasses.

"What does he mean?" Charlotte asked. "I can hug him? How?"

"No." Ty shook his head. "It's too difficult. You would need to be really willing and open to letting a spirit in."

"I'm open." She couldn't say it fast enough. "I'm willing. I want to feel him one more time. Just once. Maybe then, I can have some closure."

"I don't know," said Ty. "This kind of thing gets really personal sometimes."

"So you've done it before?"

"It doesn't always work. Sometimes I try to let in one spirit and then the people complain that it didn't feel like their loved one." He rolled his eyes. "Then they want a refund, and I'm not about to give—"

"I won't ask for a refund. Just let me feel him. Let me hold him." Charlotte moved from the couch to the floor. Dorito crumbs crunched under her knees, but she didn't care. "I *need* this."

"Okay then." Ty shrugged. "Your call, boss." He placed his hands on the planchette. "Let's see what we can do."

Charlotte's fingers joined his.

"Devon. I summon thee to present yourself."

"Devon isn't the type to come when called," Charlotte said. "Try a softer tone. Devon? Baby? I want you to hold me."

The triangular piece of wood shifted. Charlotte smiled as it spelled out: *Not alone.*

"I think he wants some privacy," Ty said.

"What?" Charlotte kept her fingers on the wood. "What if it means *he's* not alone? Like what if there's another ghost in here?"

Ty stood up. "I've had this happen before. Trust me. He wants to have you alone."

"Why?" Charlotte's hands trembled.

Ty backed away toward the bedroom in the back.

"I can't do this alone," she said.

"All you have to do is close your eyes."

Okay. I can do this. Charlotte followed instructions and shut her eyes as Ty backed away.

"Stay open and willing to let him in." His voice grew distant.

Charlotte kept her focus on the Ouija board. "Devon? Are you still here?"

The click of a door closing turned her attention away from the board. Ty had closed himself in the bedroom.

The planchette wouldn't move. She gave it a shake, hoping to wake it up somehow. "Devon? I'm here, Baby."

Nothing. "It's not working," she called out.

"Give it time!" Ty shouted from the back room. "Quiet now. Be open to his request. *Think* about him. Think about his touch."

Charlotte dusted the crumbs off her knees and sat back on the couch with her eyes closed. His silky smooth face. His laugh. She opened her heart and mind and waited for him to do something.

A gentle brush of her hair—like a warm breeze had moved her dark curls away from her ear. She shuddered at the sensation and opened her eyes.

"Devon?" she whispered. "I'm here, Baby."

A touch to her hand. Charlotte jerked away, but she was alone. Her pulse skipped as she tried to stay relaxed. Shutting her eyes again, she sat up straight and released a deep breath.

Fingers ran along her arm, prickling her skin to attention.

"Devon?" Tears filled her eyes. "Talk to me." She looked around the room, hoping he'd flicker a light or move the planchette, but he wouldn't speak.

A warm sensation ran along her collar bone, then her ear. Her thigh. The touches were everywhere. "Devon, baby, slow down. Talk to me."

An impossibly real sensation, as if a warm body was in the room with her. When she reached for him, her hands fell on empty space. His eager spirit wouldn't let up. Hot lips pressed against her. Thin lips. The scruff of facial hair on her neck.

Not Devon! Charlotte leapt from the couch and crossed her arms over her body. That wasn't Devon at all. Not even mustache-Devon. Mustache Devon wasn't prickly. Her knees trembled.

Not alone. She staggered back and bumped her head against the shelf of oddities over the mantle. The jars filled with pink-tinged formaldehyde rattled. A Barbie doll tipped over. Behind it, sat a hand-sized crocheted doll. A portly and pasty doll with wire-rimmed glasses sewn to its face. It wore a tiny grey hoodie, like the one Ty wore. Greasy dark hair sprouted from the top of its head—real human hair. Ty's hair. Between its legs, was a thumb-sized crocheted penis.

"What the fu—"

The touch of a hand sliding along Charlotte's hip caught her off-guard. Another hand on her breast.

Charlotte fumbled into her purse for her pen-knife and popped the cap off.

Facial hair scratched at her skin along her collar bone and breast. Then down her belly.

Not Devon.

She swung the knife through the air as if she could stab at the invisible force who was violating her. With her free hand, she swatted at her body, but the feeling wouldn't stop.

"Devon, help me," she whispered, chin quivering.

Ty.

Charlotte hurried toward the back bedroom while groping hands grazed her body. She flung open the door. A tiger tapestry hung on the wall over a twin-sized bed. On his hands and knees with his pants undone, Ty jerked to attention. "I'm sorry!" he shouted.

Beneath him, propped up on pillows, lay a life-sized blow-up doll. Her eyes and mouth locked in a state of surprise.

Charlotte's face matched the dolls as her jaw dropped. Eyes peeled as if opening them wider might reveal something other than a blow-up sex doll wearing her leopard jacket.

"What the hell?" she screamed.

"That was supposed to be locked!" Ty tucked his erection back into his pants and crawled out of bed.

Duct-taped to the top of the doll's head, was a tuft of black curly hair—Charlotte's hair. A shriek skittered up out of her core and pierced the dank air of Ty's bedroom. Along with it, came the puke she couldn't hold back this time.

The wide-eyed inflatable Charlotte thing just stared into space, just as disgusted that Ty's hands were touching her. All she could think to do in the moment, other than stab Ty, was to make it so he couldn't use that blow-up doll any more. Charlotte charged. She jabbed her blade into the leg of the doll.

Upon impact, a sharp stabbing pain bit her leg and she buckled to the floor, screaming.

"Oh shit," Ty said.

Charlotte pulled the knife from the doll's leg. Immediate relief from the pain, but something was still off. She lost all feeling in her leg.

Blow-up Charlotte hissed, deflating.

"What's happening?" She coughed.

"Uhhh…" Ty held up his hands, darting eyes back and forth. "I can fix it."

He pulled a roll of duct tape from the bed post and ripped a piece off with his teeth.

Charlotte crumpled to the floor, coughing. Air seemed too thin. She pulled in a breath that refused to fill her lungs.

Blow-up Charlotte deflated.

Ty pressed his duct tape onto the stab wound of the doll and pulled an air pump from the end of the bed. He attached the pump, turned on the switch, and blow-up Charlotte filled with life-saving air.

Charlotte clawed at her chest, took a short breath, but it wasn't enough.

"I'm sorry!" Ty said through tears.

As the doll inflated, Charlotte gasped, finally pulling in some air. "What's happening?" she managed to eke out.

"Voodoo. I'm sorry."

"What?"

"I learned it in Haiti. I've never had *this* happen." Ty held the hand of the blow up doll.

Charlotte sensed his touch in her palm. "Stop touching me!"

Ty pulled his hand away, palms up.

"So Devon? He was never here?" Charlotte's strength returned. Her grip adjusted around her pen-knife.

Ty sobbed as he closed the plug to the doll and turned off the pump. Charlotte charged at him with her knife. He crumpled into a pasty pile of pathetic blubber, sobbing hysterically. "No. I'm so sorry."

She pointed her knife toward his face. "What were you going to do to me?"

He had no response other than uncontrollable crying.

"You've done this to other women, haven't you?" She jabbed the knife within an inch of his face. "You voodoo rape women and tell them it was a ghost!"

A string of cotton-mouthed saliva strung from his lips. Snot poured from his nose. Ty curled in the fetal position at Charlotte's mercy.

"Undo that doll. Make it so it's not *me* anymore."

Ty obeyed. Hunched like Igor, he pulled the taped hair from her head. Charlotte snatched it away. He slid the jacket from the doll and handed it over. Back to cowering, Ty said, "I'm sorry."

"Shut up!" Charlotte wiped her tears away. Devon was right, someone should've cut that guy's dick off a long time ago.

Through the blur of tears in her eyes, she held Ty at knife point while he whimpered.

She couldn't bring herself to do it though. She couldn't kill him. Or stab him.

Instead, she ran. On her way out she grabbed her purse and paused by the shelf of oddities.

Go get what you want, girl. Devon's voice—or maybe his spirit—spoke to her. She *wanted* to protect other woman from this monster. She *wanted* revenge.

Charlotte escaped the house, but stood for a moment on Ty's front porch to release a held breath. It was as if she'd been holding it since Devon died. She'd have to deal with the fact that she'd never have Devon back. She'd never hold him again, or hear his laugh. As she exhaled, she set free the mountain of ash that had collected inside her. Even without her Devon, there could still be purpose in her life.

In her hand, she held the small crocheted doll with the wire-rimmed glasses and the disproportioned penis. The one that resembled Ty.

She plunged her razor-sharp knife into the crocheted doll... for the sake of humanity.

A bellow bled through the walls of Ty's house. A screech of agony like she'd never heard. He'd never be able to impose himself on a woman again.

As Charlotte stepped off the porch, a thumb-sized, crocheted penis fell to the ground.

ODOR MORTIS

HAROLD SLITHERED the tip of his nose along the body, absorbing the scent into his soul until he was gravid with pleasure. A female, mid-thirties, graced the table in his basement embalming room. Being a mortician allowed him to keep his fervor for a corpse's acrid aroma a secret from the public.

Like any other person, he spent his evenings watching shows while swiping left on a dating app. Most women, he assumed, had no interest in coming back to his place considering he lived in his funeral home. A lack of confidence, and fear they'd discover his unorthodox delights in the fragrantly deceased, kept Harold from ever reaching out to the women on the app.

He preferred the people on the table to the living anyway.

A tragic car accident landed the current body into his caring hands. A wreck mangled the right half of her face beyond recognition. Harold was smitten by what was left of her. A remaining soft, black eyebrow, slick to the touch like a crow's feather, framed the woman's left eye. She had a kind eye, one that he could stare into all day. Pale skin contrasted thick, dark hair. As Harold leaned his face against her cheek and inhaled, he was reminded of his childhood friend, Jenna. Had she been given the chance to grow up, Jenna would have looked like the woman on his table.

When they were ten years old, Harold and Jenna had been walking down the country road, singing and laughing under the summer sun. The roar of a speeding vehicle had approached so fast, before Harold had a chance to see it coming, Jenna was struck. Her body flipped into the air and crashed to the gravel shoulder. The truck slowed, but then sped away never to be found.

Harold cradled Jenna's broken body. As he waited for a passerby, she grew heavier and blood absorbed through the cotton of her yellow sundress. Sweaty arms clung to her lifeless form. His tear-soaked cheeks pressed against her blood and gravel-splattered face. He embraced his best friend and begged for her to be alright, but on this stretch of country road nobody was coming to help.

Then he detected it.

At first he turned away from the foreign, pungent odor, but he was intrigued. Having never smelled anything like it, he leaned in for another sniff. Fighting a natural response to reject the odor, he dove in for more. The fragrance had filled his nostrils, caressing his olfactory receptors, and smothered the tips of his taste buds. Harold liked to think that part of Jenna's soul had stayed with him that day, respired into his body with each mournful breath.

He traced his finger along the cadaver's brow bone, astonished by her resemblance to Jenna. The mangled half of her face had been fixed with stitches and makeup to the best of his ability. He brushed her thick, black hair over her mutilated half. Because of her disfigurement, the family had requested a closed-casket funeral, but he wasn't preparing her for *them*. It would be a pity to embalm her, especially if nobody would see her.

Harold laid her nude body on his bed. Gases attempted their escape from the fleshy confines, bloating her and making the fetor even more intoxicating. From a plastic bag, he pulled a new yellow sundress. He slid the cotton over her swollen feet, gliding the fabric along her pale, blue legs and around her hips. The warm, sunny cotton masked her olive green, distended belly. Harold supported her head, hoisted her torso up against himself, and respectfully shroud her breasts within the garment.

She rested peacefully on his bed while he slipped under the covers alongside her. Cold fingers welcomed his warm touch as he inserted his hand into hers. He lay next to her, reminiscing of their summers playing together, talking about his day and how happy she made him. The bed would shake from Harold's laughter, erupting plumes of putrid perfume into the air.

He kept his old friend company each night. Coagulated blood settled into her back and buttocks. Her eyeballs shriveled behind closed lids. Weeks passed and the bouquet changed. No worse, nor better, but different. Her body broke down, releasing a slow leak of new chemicals. An evolution of essential odors, each stage as perfect as the next. Life couldn't be any better. But all things that bring happiness eventually get taken.

Over time, the remains of what used to be Jenna (or the woman that could have been Jenna) were sticky and skeletal. The aroma of decay waned and Harold's gut gurgled with a hunger for more. He twitched, scratching at his arms. Ever since his new Jenna came along, none of the other bodies that came through his funeral home satisfied him. Jenna's face was a frosting on his fetish that he couldn't go without.

But she was rotting away.

Waiting for another closed-casket victim that looked like his best friend could take a lifetime. He couldn't risk the wait.

He kissed the exposed skull on her forehead and promised he'd find her again. After inhaling the remnants of Jenna's musk, he went to the living room and opened his dating app. Repeated left swipes revealed a multitude of disappointing options. Blurred faces (all the wrong faces) passed by. Persevering through his search for over an hour, he began to lose hope. As exhaustion took over and he began to nod off, a pale face with dark hair caught his attention. His pulse hitched with the prospect that he found her.

A woman with dark brows and kind eyes had a coy smile. She would be perfect for him, but first he would need to release her morbid fragrance.

SLICE

WHOEVER THOUGHT KANGAROO meat would make a good topping for pizza must've been high. Based on the appearance of the old woman behind the counter, Tara was surprised they didn't have alligator or moose-butt on the toppings list. The woman, with her face gnarled into a perpetual state of disgust, stared at the girls while they ate.

"What's up with the Russian pizza wench?" Marissa whispered.

Tara shrugged. Earlier, she had suggested they eat somewhere else—perhaps the place in Times Square—but Marissa had her heart set on the filthiest, hole-in-the-wall joint she could find. Tucked at the end of a garbage-scented alley, and with no neon lights to guide them to it, Grisha's Pizza was way off the beaten path.

"That's why we're here," Marissa said with a wad of pizza in the side of her cheek. "To try new things." She took a bite of the limp, oversized slice. "Oh that's weird."

"Fine." Tara caved, and set down her safe slice of pepperoni to try a bite of Marissa's. She chomped into the grease-soaked slice and a chunk of kangaroo fell apart in her mouth. It slid down her throat with ease. "Actually, that's kind of good."

Marissa threw her arms in the air in celebration. "You did it! You actually tried something new." She leaned in closer. "Now we just have to get you laid."

A pizza shop employee, sweeping near their table, stumbled over his own feet. Naturally, this sent Marissa into a hysterical episode of laughter. "I think we shocked the poor guy. Maybe you and him can—"

"Shhh! Don't even say it."

"—do it." Marissa thrusted her hips within her seat.

"How about we find jobs first," Tara said.

"Boris!" The haggardly Russian woman shouted from behind the counter, then followed up with a string of Russian words.

Marissa whispered across the table, "Can you imagine having sex with a Boris. Oh Boris, Boris!"

"Shut up," Tara laughed.

Boris had to be in his early twenties, shaggy, in a filthy kind of way. He kept his head down as he was summoned

145

behind the counter. The two spoke quietly in Russian, in an obvious discussion about Tara and Marissa. Behind them, hung a gold-framed old-timey photograph of a man. Eyes lost in the blackness of the antique photo's shadowy contrast, they seemed to stare at Tara as she took another bite of pizza—or perhaps his eyes were lost under his massive unibrow.

"So weird," Tara mumbled.

"This pizza is weirder," Marissa said slapping the half-eaten slice onto her plate. "Trade?"

They swapped slices, scarfed down their lunch, and while tossing out their garbage, the Russian woman approached them. "You girls need job?"

Boris interjected, arguing with the woman in their native tongue, but she cut him off with some sharp words.

"No," Tara said. "We're good."

Marissa shot her a glare.

"I hear you say you need job," the Russian woman said.

Behind the woman, Boris shook his head as if warning Tara of something. For a moment, Tara was insulted that he didn't want them employed at Grisha's, but then it made sense. *Roaches.* There had to be a nasty infestation of cockroaches for the guy to be so adamant about them not accepting a job. The little critters had to be all over the kitchen—or maybe it was rats. Tara shivered.

"Yeah, we need job," Marissa said, mocking the woman's accent. "I worked at Gino's back home. We made our own dough and our own sauce—"

"*We* make our own sauce!" The woman interjected, lip curling in disgust.

If Boris was able to shoot daggers from his eyes, Tara was certain he was about to do it. His glare pierced her with an intense but silent warning to leave.

"Great," Marissa said. "So I won't need much training."

Tara cringed. "I'm not sure about th—"

"You start now," the woman said and held out a grease-stained apron. "Both of you work. I pay cash. No taxes."

The woman's eyebrows arched as if Tara should've been impressed with the offer to work under the table.

Marissa's face couldn't hide her excitement, and before Tara could argue, they were employees of Grisha's Pizza. *Just like that.* There wasn't much to argue about though. They would both work for a few hours and walk out with cash in hand, despite the roaches, rats, or whatever horrors lurked in the kitchen that Boris did not want them to see.

"I'm Zlata, Grisha's great granddaughter," she held her chin high, pointing her thumb to the man in the old photo— unibrow man. "This place is Grisha's passion. They say the oldest pizza shop is Lombardi's or Totanno's. No! It's Grisha's! His pizza sauce, his passion. We keep recipe the same all these years."

"Wow." Marissa sneered, then rolled her eyes behind Zlata's back.

Zlata faced the photograph with loving admiration. "Come. I show you the kitchen."

147

The black void where Grisha's eyes should have been followed Tara as she was led around a ceiling-high rack of pizza shelves and into the kitchen. A thickness in the air, metallic and spicy, stung her nose as she entered.

"This is the recipe," Zlata said, pointing to a framed print on the wall—edges of the old document yellowed and disintegrating. She stirred a pot of marinara simmering on a back burner. "The sauce is here. Right before it goes on pizza, you put it in the bowl and add these three things."

Three ceramic mortar and pestle dishes with crushed herbs sat in a row on the counter.

"OK," Marissa said.

Zlata leaned in closer, nearly touching Marissa's face. "*Only*, these ingredients in the sauce. Exactly! Or bad things happen."

"Jeez lady, alright," Marissa held up her hands. "I'm not in the business of getting fired. I get it."

"What do you mean, 'bad things happen?'" Tara asked with a lump of nerves caught in her throat.

Zlata shrugged. "Grisha gets upset."

After Boris gave her a brief training on the register, Tara had the job down, but couldn't shake the feeling that the antique photograph of Grisha was watching her.

Grisha gets upset—what the hell was that supposed to mean? The crazy bitch had Tara on edge. As soon as she had her opportunity for a break, she planned to get out of there.

148

Tara took orders, dishing out slices and ringing up the few people that came, and for a few hours, Zlata scolded Marissa over too much oregano or not enough garlic. Eventually, Marissa must've gotten it right, because Zlata eased off.

After serving the last slice of kangaroo-topped pizza to a brave college guy, I let Marissa know that we were out.

Marissa looked to Zlata, who was watching her every move.

Zlata shook her head. "What? You think we have kangaroos hopping around out back? No more until the next shipment comes. Take it off the menu."

"Look, we have to leave soon," Marissa said. "Can we get paid?"

Zlata went to the register, counted out some bills and slapped them into Tara's hand. "Come back. I pay again tomorrow. But first, I go smoke." Zlata stopped in the doorway and reminded Marissa, "*Only* the recipe."

"Alright!" Marissa snapped. "I got it now."

Once Zlata had left the kitchen with Boris for a cigarette, Marissa said, "It's hotter'n hell back here."

"Let's get out of here. I'm not coming back."

Marissa peeked her head through the opening in the pizza shelves to make eye contact with Tara, then in a bad Russian accent, said, "Yes. But first, I stick to the recipe." A devious smile crept across her face and she darted to the back counter for a salt shaker. "Too much salt. Not enough garlic." Marissa shook the seasoning into the small bowl of sauce with the flamboyance of a mad scientist.

Tara shook her head laughing. A violent click from the front door startled her. An empty lobby—but the deadbolt had been turned.

Marissa spooned the sauce onto the crust with a fake, maniacal laugh. "Grisha get upset," Marissa mocked.

Tara walked around the counter to the lobby with Grisha's blackened eye sockets following her. The condensing air stung her eyes as she edged toward the front door. Fluorescent lights flickered overhead.

"Marissa!" she said. "Let's go."

"Sounds good to me."

Tara, from across the lobby, listened as Marissa shoved the pizza into the fiery brick oven. Flames whooshed, casting a flash of orange light across the walls.

"Holy sh—" Marissa said. The oven door slammed shut. "That's gotta be an OSHA hazard or something."

Tara grabbed the lock of the deadbolt, but it wouldn't budge. She cranked harder. Lights dimmed. She whipped around to see Grisha staring back at her through the photograph. His visage illuminated by an inexplicable light source over his head.

"Marissa!" Tara ran behind the counter, pulse quickening. "Now." She bent down to peek through the opening in the shelves.

Backed against the stainless steel counter with her hands up, Marissa shifted her eyes toward Tara.

"What's wrong?" As soon as the words left Tara's mouth, she knew. Flames in the brick oven raged, seeping from the poorly sealed oven door, while Marissa stood frozen against the counter.

Three pizza slicers hung in the air before Marissa. Nobody held them. No strings. No explanation for the three objects to animate and hold her friend hostage—no explanation other than *Grisha got upset*.

His photograph morphed in the flickering light, laughing, taunting.

Then as time seemed to pause, Tara's pulse slowed. Blood thickening, she walked around the shelves toward the kitchen.

Gleaming, spinning blades levitated before Marissa, who was still petrified, hands up. Tara took a step closer to her friend. "You'll fix the recipe, right?"

"What?" Marissa asked, shaking her head.

"Grisha is upset," Tara said. "Fix the sauce."

"I already put it in the oven," Marissa said out of the side of her mouth. "What's happening?"

"We'll fix it," Tara said.

Marissa shuffled closer to Tara.

"Don't move," Tara urged. "I'll fix it."

Marissa darted toward the exit anyway. But not fast enough.

The shrill metallic sound of the pizza cutters sliced the air. Before Tara could blink, it was too late. Three simultaneous attacks of the slicers, and Marissa dropped to her knees.

A moment later, a thin line of red seeped through Marissa's shirt. Then another. The cuts stretched across her abdomen, oozing massive amounts of blood. She grabbed at her belly, unable to stop the bleeding with her hands. Blood spilled between her fingers. Marissa opened her mouth, but nothing came out.

"It'll be okay," Tara said, collapsing to her knees before her friend, unsure how to help. "I'll fix it." Focused on the blood pouring from Marissa's gut, Tara hadn't seen the third wound. The papercut-thin gash in Marissa's throat finally opened up, spewing blood down her chest, and her body crumpled into a pile on the dirty ceramic tiles.

Tara squealed, gasping for her breath. She hovered over Marissa with tremoring hands. There was no time. Blood-dripping pizza cutters drifted toward her. She scrambled to her feet, slipping in Marissa's blood. The haunted cutters tormented her, closing in as she backed toward the stove. Overhead lights flickered.

"I'll fix it," she whispered. Shaking hands fumbled with the ingredients to make a new batch of sauce as Grisha watched over her carefully. "I'll fix it," she repeated. Tears blurred her vision, making the recipe too difficult to read. The tinny sound of the spinning blades assaulted her ears as she trembled. She prepared the sauce as directed.

"She didn't follow the recipe!" Zlata shouted as she and Boris came back from their break, entering the kitchen to a blood-soaked body. "Grisha," she sighed, and spoke more words in Russian to her great-grandfather.

Tara, eyes burning and heart shattered, frantically spooned the sauce onto the next pie. Her gut churned as she choked back the vomit that tried to escape. Spinning blades of the cutters edged closer to her face, but she kept working, determined not to upset Grisha again. "I'll fix it," she promised.

Tara pulled the burned pizza from the fire and tossed it into the garbage. After sliding the properly prepared pizza into the brick oven, Tara held her breath, awaiting her fate.

The pizza cutters backed off and rested themselves on the counter.

Boris grabbed hold of Marissa's arms and tugged at her body. He dragged her toward the back room, while Zlata held the door open to assist. Knees weak, Tara crouched down, slowly collapsing to the floor and sobbing as her friend's body was dragged into the back.

As the door swung shut, Zlata's voice carried through. "Looks like tomorrow we have..." She raised her hands for air quotes. "... *kangaroo* on the menu again."

Boris shook his head while Zlata chuckled, leaving Tara crumpled over a pool of her friend's blood.

INTIMIDATING SMILE

"NO, I'M NOT A VAMPIRE," I say to the checkout woman behind the counter.

If I had a dollar for every time I've had to say those words, I'd be rich beyond my wildest imagination. I could buy myself a massive castle in the hills of Transylvania and get away from people that ask stupid questions. *Honestly, people. Be original.*

Meaty, manicured fingers hand me a white plastic bag with my purchase inside. The checkout woman at the mall I rarely go to stares like I'm lying. One too many YA novels probably has her thinking there's an underground clan of werewolves too in this town.

"Well," she says with a smile. "I think your fangs are cool. Makes you one of a kind."

I'm tired of people staring. It's never just one person. Tonight, it was the checkout woman and a weirdo in a canvas coat. He turned up in every aisle of the book store. I bet he wants a glimpse of my teeth. They always do. I won't be surprised if he comes up to me any minute and asks to take a selfie with me. Some of the real freaks want me to *bite* them. And it wouldn't be the first time I've been asked to do that. How many seventeen year olds have to put up with this kind of behavior?

I'm so ready for a change.

The doctors call my condition hypohidrotic ectodermal dysplasia. Mom calls it my *special gift*. What kind of gift is this? I would rather have gotten a puppy. The doctors said that I'm lucky it isn't worse. *Ha! Lucky!* Most people with this condition go bald, so I'm *lucky* that I have hair. Even if it's a little thin.

I'm *lucky* that my intolerance to heat hasn't caused a seizure yet—only a few minor blackouts. And I'm *lucky* that I have all of my teeth. It's common for people like me to have pointed, but few teeth. Apparently it's inconsequential to the doctors that—even though my teeth are in good condition—my canine teeth are long and pointed. Not only do they cause callouses on the inside of my lips, but they also instill fear into everyone I meet.

I can be in the same room with a crowd for hours, not once trying to suck their blood, and all it takes is a simple smile. One smile from a pale young girl, exposing a set of sharp fangs, and their perception of who I am changes in an instant. I become either the most vile thing ever, or the most perversely fascinating thing to them. *People are gross.*

The teeth need to go. They have been undoubtedly *un*lucky.

We think it's hereditary. My mother told me that she only knew my dad *about a hot minute* before they did the deed that led to me. *Classy, Mom.* Don't people have standards?

"Well, he was missing some teeth," she admitted with a shrug. "But he never mentioned a condition. In fact, he blacked out right after we... you know."

Gross. There's an image I can't ever get out of my head, even if I never actually saw it happen. The point is, my father was likely the carrier of this condition, even if he didn't know he had it. He passed it on to me. Seriously, the worst hand-me-down genes ever.

Mom boasts that I came into this world ready to take a bite out of life. She's so lame. I wish she'd stop saying that. My father, on the other hand—upon my arrival coated in placental gook, caterwauling from between my baby fangs—believed me to be the spawn of Satan. He ran for the hills—possibly the ones in Transylvania, since that seems to be the fabled place where people like us come from. I'd better rethink my plan for spending my hypothetical money on that castle there. I have no interest in meeting good ol' bio-dad.

The freak in the canvas coat, who was staring, peeks over his shoulder as he leaves the store ahead of me. Maybe he's not the type that wants a selfie. Nope. He's the type that's afraid of me. He hurries his pace and speeds out the door.

I reach into my pocket for Mom's Suburu keys and pull my hood up as I head to the front entrance. Cool air engulfs me as I approach the doors. I hate the cold. I wish I could lay in the sun, feel the warmth on my face without consequences. The cold is where I belong though. When I was a kid, we learned that my body couldn't sweat enough to cool itself down. After my first blackout, we were at the doctor's office.

"Not enough anti-freeze in her," the doctor joked. *Adults are so lame.* "Your skin doesn't sweat like it's supposed to."

A week later, Mom packed up her car and moved us out of the sizzling state of Texas, all the way to Alaska.

"Bigger is better," she said with proud geographic knowledge of state sizes.

I rolled my eyes, as most kids do at their parents. Mom's optimism is unbearable.

"Same goes for your teeth," she said. "Bigger is better." *Says the woman who sleeps with random toothless men.*

I have to hand it to her though, she's not too shabby at parenting and making me feel like I'm good enough as is. Talk about unconditional love. Countless hours of my teen years have been spent begging for a procedure to make these cursed teeth smaller. Maybe then, I might gain some semblance of normalcy.

"But, look at that smile," Mom always said.

"I *am* looking at it," I argued. "I just wish it was a little less... I don't know... intimidating?"

The reflection of a pale and pretty face stares back at me as I near the bookstore exit. It disappears as the automatic doors open. I've learned not to smile much in public, and that drives Mom crazy. But flashing my fangs only brings shock and awe wherever I go. I wasn't even trying to show my teeth and the intrusive checkout woman had to go and ask the million dollar question about my pointy teeth. Canvas-coat freak had to run in fear.

Intrigue and questioning. Fear and disgust. It has become far too exhausting to handle.

I can't be expected to go to college in a few months looking like this. High school was bad enough. Friends were few and far between in my small town. Many of my close friends had moved away over the years.

And don't get me going about dating. I was seeing a boy once, but his obsession with my teeth became the focus of his affection for me. Every date became about me pretending to bite him.

"Show me your teeth again," he'd say.

I drew the line at dinner with his grandmother. Here I thought he was asking me over with some level of sincerity to meet his family. He assured me that he warned them about my condition. *Nope.* As soon as I smiled and said, "Hello," to the old woman, she shrieked, made the sign of the cross and ran into the other room. My boyfriend laughed hysterically and I dumped his lame ass.

I can already imagine the freaks in college lining up to get a picture with—or worse—bitten by the vampire girl. Or maybe they'll just run away at first sight and leave me alone.

I didn't even bother applying to any of the Christian colleges. I'd likely be burned at the stake. *No, that's witches, isn't it?* Either way, it nauseates me to think that life after high school won't be any different than it is now.

People of all ages treat me the same way—like a freak.

But that's all going to change. *I'm* going to change.

In order to fix the unfortunate size of my canines, dentists would have to extract them and replace them with dental implants. That kind of procedure was never within Mom's budget. Not that she'd let me go through with it even if she could afford it.

My gift should be embraced, she'd say.

What she doesn't know, is that I've been saving my money over the past few years and I almost have enough to pay for the procedure. Mom will be devastated. I'm hopeful this little plastic bag full of her favorite incense and chocolates is enough to warm her over for when I break the news about my plans to extract my *special gift.*

The air is crisp and cold as I cross the quiet parking lot toward the car. Chunks of ice crunch beneath my feet.

I run my tongue along the tip of my canine tooth. I wonder if I'll miss them. Part of me will. That little part of me that's really okay with who I am. But the rest of me—the part that has to face the public—is sick of them.

It'll break Mom's heart.

An abrupt blow to my back knocks the wind out of me. A set of burly arms wrap around my chest and pull me backward. I gasp beneath their clutch, pulling in a sharp breath of icy air between my teeth. A hand covers my mouth as I'm dragged into a van through the side panel door. I fight, kicking and screaming. A throbbing pulse at the base of my skull blurs my vision.

The van door slides shut. Yellow parking lot lights pour through the window of the dank van. The grotesque, hairy-faced man in the canvas coat pins me on my back.

Canvas-coat freak. Hate crime?

My heart rate skyrockets. Body temperature creeps up. Vision narrows. I'm about to black out. In one last effort to escape, I do all I can think to do. All my fear and wrath unleashes in a guttural growl. I growl into the man's face, exposing my fangs. The sound that comes out me is something I didn't know I had in me.

An ungodly fear encompasses his face.

"What the hell?" He stumbles back, staring toward my mouth.

I lunge my fangs toward his wrist, ready to bite into him. He yanks away. His eyes widen as if he was meeting the devil himself. The kind of terror I imagine my father had when I was born.

The man releases me and scurries out of the van in a panic, falling down and then scrambling back to his feet. Canvas-coat freak darts across the parking lot in a chaotic escape and disappears into the darkness. My heart pummels my ribcage. I stumble out of the van lightheaded.

I wake up in the back of an ambulance. The medics say I overheated and passed out.

"Low on anti-freeze," I explain with a straight face, and the EMT lets out a hardy laugh. I guess it's not that lame of a joke.

The police catch up with my attacker and discover that the monster is wanted in Oregon for kidnap and murder. The guy didn't know I had fangs. He didn't seek me out because I was a freak. I was just the unlucky girl that crossed his path. Mom and the sheriff commend my ability to fight the guy off, but I know it wasn't my strength that saved me.

Lucky I have these teeth. They saved my life.

I'd like to show up at that degenerate's trial, just to scare him. Perhaps if I glare at him from across the courtroom—give him a flash of my smile—it will keep him trembling in terror for the rest of his life. This defect of mine has proven useful for once. Maybe it's time that I grow up and try to embrace it.

THE ASTRONOMER'S MISTRESS

THOMAS WAITED FOR HIS WIFE to say something but she didn't move. Tears welled within her eyes, and the reflection of the fireplace in her watery gaze burned his heart.

"It's a rose," Thomas said. "Roses are your favorite."

The framed photograph of one of his favorite celestial objects nearly made him cry when it came back from the printer, so he was not surprised Marilyn was stunned by its beauty.

"Starshine, are you all right?" Thomas placed a gentle hand on Marilyn's arm.

"Don't call me that." She tugged away from him and her black chiffon robe, studded with silver stars, slid beneath his fingers.

"It's a term of endearment." His eyes shifted to the anniversary gift in her hands. "That's the Rosette Nebula. I've been imaging it for you. That's why I've been out back in the observatory so much lately. I know you get upset when I spend too much time out there, but I've been picking you a rose." His confidence faded with each passing second. "You see, it's a cloud of gas over five thousand light years away where stars are forming. Look at the shape. It's like a rose."

"That's not a rose," she said through clenched teeth.

"Sure it is, just look—"

"You're always out there in that shed."

"But this time it was for you." Thomas feigned a smile.

"This present is not for *me*."

"Of course it is. I spent hours on that."

"You spent hours with *her* again, didn't you?"

"With who?" Thomas asked, puzzled by the accusation and laughing at the notion of having an affair at his age.

"Don't play stupid!" In a swift outburst, Marilyn tossed the photograph of the Rosette Nebula into the fireplace. The glass shattered against brick.

"What are you doing?" He pushed by her and fumbled his arthritic fingers around the handle of the fire poker, jabbing at the photograph in the back of the fireplace, frantic to save his work. Once he caught the frame on the hook of the poker, he pulled it out and dropped it onto the hearth. It warped and bubbled, and bits of hot red ash fizzled at his feet.

Dumbfounded by his wife's actions, Thomas assessed the damage and then—to keep from raising his voice—stormed out of the house and into the backyard, heading for his sanctuary.

He unlatched the roof of the shed and rolled it back to expose the stars. The constellation Orion sparkled high in a January sky. Earlier that evening, he wasn't sure if the clouds would clear out. At the Lakeside Bistro, he and Marilyn had watched the sunset over the water. They drank in the reds and purples of the setting sun while Thomas secretly wished for the scattered clouds to go away. The sky had granted him his wish. If only Marilyn was as understanding of his needs.

She had told him last year that if he didn't start getting things right soon, their relationship would be over. Empty threats, considering they had been together for forty years. However, he wanted to make her happy, so this year he made a real effort.

He was certain last year's extravagant bouquet of stargazer lilies wouldn't compare to this single rose. Neither would the lightweight hatchet engraved with her favorite constellation, Orion. Marilyn had complained that their woodcutting axe was getting too heavy for her, so Thomas thought the hatchet would be the perfect gift. Marilyn was not impressed.

This day and this image of the Rosette Nebula was supposed to bury all the other gifts in infamy and rekindle the starry-eyed wonder that used to spark in Marilyn's eyes when she looked at him. He had contended with clouds and atmospheric disturbances for weeks. Thomas stacked hundreds of images, taken on several different days, dealing with cooling issues and alignment problems. If only she understood how much work he put into her Rosette image, perhaps she'd be more appreciative.

He looked to the constellation above as if the archer in the sky was his best friend. "What does she mean, *'it's not for her?'*" Thomas slid his arms into the warmth of his fleece jacket, took a seat beside his telescope and leaned back for a view of his stars. They were his haven—his constant. Dazzling and brilliant lights pulled his thoughts away, and he was able to catch his breath and calm down. Starlight reached out to him from light years away and caressed his soul. His sky was always there for him, even when Marilyn was not. As his blood pressure lowered, he relaxed within the walls of his observatory, beneath his stars, and let his petty problems melt away—until he heard the sound of the storm door on the house slamming shut.

Thomas stepped outside into the blackness of the night. Nothing but starlight above and a faint yellow glow came from the house windows.

"Marilyn?"

There was no response other than the crepitation of a branch in the woods. Two days ago, she had been out in the woods for hours, then came back filthy and distraught. She had said she got lost out there, which was out of character for Marilyn. Thomas wondered if her mind was fading—early signs of dementia, perhaps.

"Thomas?" The soft broken words came from the forest. Marilyn's star-studded robe was easy to spot against the blackness of the tree line.

"What on earth are you doing?" he asked.

Darkness concealed the rest of her body from sight as her sparkling robe flowed into the woods.

Thomas walked to the edge of the tree line, and Marilyn faded as she drew deeper into the dense forest.

"Thomas?"

"I'm right here! Are you going senile?" He stomped into the woods. Guided by the ghostly movement of her robe in the distance, Thomas strained to keep sight of her. He pulled his red LED flashlight from his pocket and aimed it in the direction he had last seen her. The faint crimson glow of his astronomer's flashlight—colored to protect his view of the dark sky—revealed nothing but crowded trees and forest floor shrubbery.

"Marilyn? Dang it! Where are you?"

The sound of movement—dead soggy leaves—startled him, and a swift shine of his red light illuminated the bare branches and tangles of underbrush, but no Marilyn.

Thomas's heart raced as he took careful footsteps over fallen twigs and brush, wondering where his wife had gone. Maybe she really was having some issues with early senility.

"Starshine? Follow my voice if you can hear me!"

As he shone his light ahead, he spotted a dark patch on the ground. The splotch of blackness about the size of a bear stopped him. The brush crunched behind him and he whipped his head around, shining the red light in the sound's direction.

Thomas shifted his gaze back to the bear-like mass, but it hadn't moved.

A closer investigation of the dark patch of ground did not reveal a sleeping bear but a mound of dirt, several feet tall. Beside it, a shallow uneven trench dug into the earth. Worried Marilyn may have stumbled into it, he edged closer.

"Starshine?" he whispered.

Another foot closer exposed a shovel sticking out of the mound—*his* shovel.

"I said don't call me that!" Marilyn's voice came from behind, along with a sudden sharp blast to his lower back. Thomas crumbled to his knees. A rush of heat flooded his spine, and spiky needle-like pain sparked like fireworks across his body. Face-first, he fell to the ground, his nose pressed against the sodden, moldy leaves. Red light skimmed across the surface of the damp earth and the flashlight fell still. With a swift thwack, a hatchet covered in his blood lodged into the ground beside him. Engraved on the handle was the constellation Orion. His vision tunneled to darkness as dainty loafers stepped into his view.

"Marilyn?" he muttered, barely able to get it out before losing consciousness.

Thomas's vision blurred into focus to reveal the bright unmistakable stars of Orion. Assuming he had fallen asleep in his observatory, he sighed in relief that the nightmare was over. But that peaceful, ephemeral thought ended as his eyes adjusted to see tree branches snaking black jagged interruptions in the sky. Unable to shift his shoulders between the soil walls entrapping him, Thomas realized he was at the bottom of the trench.

He tried to get to his feet, but his legs were unresponsive to his commands. His nerves, deadened by the blow to his spinal cord, refused to react.

"Marilyn?" The warmth of his blood absorbing into the back of his shirt made him sick to his stomach. White-hot pain throbbed deep, burning like the core of the sun, and skittered to the surface of his skin in undulant flares.

A star-studded robe floated into view up above, like a globular cluster of stars. Marilyn held the robe in one hand, four feet above him, with Thomas's shovel in the other hand.

"Marilyn." His lips lost feeling as he dribbled out her name. A piercing pain shot down his neck.

The robe drifted softly on the cold air down into the pit, reminding him of the first time she had slipped it on. The starry robe that—even at his age—made him want to be intimate. He had bought it for her. For *her*—but she had argued otherwise. It landed on his hands which were rested on his belly, losing strength.

"I told you. You had one more chance to get it right," she said, standing at the edge of the pit.

"I worked hard on that picture. For *you*," Thomas said with difficulty. His strength escaped him, absorbing into the earth with his blood.

"That was not for me," she said. "*You* love the stars. I asked for one thing that's for me, and you couldn't do it. Even today—our anniversary—you couldn't stop looking at the sky. The sunset captivated you more than I could ever." She pointed up and her voice rattled. "You have spent more time with *her* over the last forty years than you have with me."

"I—" Thomas fought to speak, but the words caught in his throat.

"I warned you." She dropped the hatchet into the hole, and it lodged into the ground beside his face.

Sparks shot through the nerve endings in his spine and down into his fingertips. A need to fight back swelled within—to argue that she never appreciated the things he did for her. His time under the stars was well-spent, and if she had only opened her eyes, she would have experienced the beauty of the entire universe. Instead, Marilyn, like so many others, confine their interests to this single pale blue dot. With saliva strung between his lips, he forced out the only words he could manage—the only words that mattered.

"I love you, Marilyn."

"But you love *her* more." She grabbed a handful of dirt and chucked it into the hole at Thomas's face. Another handful smacked him in the chest, but his nerve endings failed him and barely registered the impact. Marilyn used the shovel to dump a pile of dirt onto his belly. "This is your fault!"

The cold, damp earth fell onto his gut and plumed into clouds of petrichor, reminding him of Marilyn's scent after she'd been gardening. He couldn't muster the strength to move his arms out from under it. Beneath the loose soil, his fingers brushed against the soft chiffon.

He looked back to the sky.

"Stop looking at her!" Marilyn got on her hands and knees to push mounds of dirt into his grave.

Guttural sobs from above, interrupted by the wet thuds of earth.

The sound of her weeping and the sound of the falling dirt blended in a sorrowful pulsing song. As soil and rock piled onto him, his body betrayed his fight to escape and went numb. All limbs lost sensation and he could no longer palpate that soft chiffon with his fingertips.

Questions and unfinished business raced through his mind and heart. A desire to fight for his life, and to fight for his wife's love, coursed through him, but he was trapped. Defenseless, he locked his eyes on the glorious light shining from the stars, Betelgeuse, Rigel, and Sirius. The starlight penetrated his heart and whispered to him that he'd be all right. It traveled across the galaxy just for Thomas, to comfort him in his last moment, so he listened.

"Look at me!" Marilyn used her body to bulldoze a mound of dirt into his grave, this time concealing his mouth and nose.

Paralyzed and losing life, Thomas pulled in scant amounts of oxygen through his one exposed nostril.

"Look at me." Her voice hitched and choked upon sobs.

Thomas could not break his fixated gaze. The sparkling gems against the blackness of the night shone on him with more love than he could ever reciprocate. Peripheral vision lost sight of Marilyn, and her voice was silenced by a static. With a content heart, he looked to his love—the stars—one last time, and his vision went black.

MEMORY LANE

A BABY'S LAUGH PLAYED on repeat when Victor pressed the button. She giggled, then rocketed to a high pitched coo, and back down to a stuttering laugh—like a song. A recording of Hayden's voice was locked into the yellow cover of a photo album, pages empty beyond eleven months.

Victor pressed the button again. *Giggle-coo-laugh.*

Again...

Around the edge of the plastic button, years of wear rubbed the cover bare.

He sipped from a mug and wished it were gin, but he gave that up years ago, right after he lost her to that damn drunk driver.

Victor pressed it again, but the recording slowed.

Again. It deepened and dragged. The giggle-coo saddened into a slow, manly drawl, and then the battery quit for good.

He pressed it again. Nothing.

Again... Silence.

A desperate finger pressed harder and harder, but Hayden couldn't talk to him anymore.

Victor rocked, head clamped between his hands, squeezing tufts of hair through his fingers.

"Victor," his wife Elena's voice rang. "Take these. It'll help." She pushed two small pills in front of him.

He swatted them away and they flung to the floor.

"Victor!"

He folded over in his chair and crumpled to the floor under the table, with Hayden's photo album against his chest.

"I need her back," he whispered. "Please. I need to hear her voice. Please. *Please*..."

He swayed in the painful silence.

Hidden beneath the draped shelter of a tablecloth, Victor prayed. "I'll give anything," he whispered, "just to hear her voice."

Guttural moans of despair spilled from his core. Saliva strung between his lips. Victor begged for help from Heaven, or from Hell, or from whomever would listen.

Something nudged his knee, and when he opened his eyes, a girl, no more than ten years old, pushed a blue photo album, much like his own, into his leg.

Victor scrambled backward up against the table leg, but she tilted her head and smiled.

"You can hear her laugh again if you take this." Her scrawny arms swam in a gray jersey as she held the album out for Victor.

He hesitated. "Who are you?" Her eyes were like Elena's—warm and kind, heavy lashes.

"Press the button," she said.

Victor reached for the book and pushed on the round plastic button.

Giggle-coo-laugh.

His shoulders relaxed with the glorious sound of Hayden's laugh.

As Victor tried to grab it, the young girl pulled it back. "This photo album is not just what *was*, but it's also what could have been."

"What do you mean?"

She opened the book.

Twelve Months: A birthday photo shoot with a big number one. Balloons. A picture of his daughter with cake and frosting smeared all over her face.

Victor's weeping turned to laughter. "There's another button," he said.

The girl in the gray jersey nodded with a grin. "Press it."

I yuv you, Dada.—the recording played.

Breath stole, Victor gaped at the impossible. He reached to turn the page, but the girl pulled the book away.

"There's a price," she said.

What price would he have to pay for such a gift? "Is it... my soul?" he asked.

"Don't be silly," she laughed. "You'll know the price when the time comes."

"Anything. I don't care." He grabbed at the book and the girl released it to him.

He flipped to the next page.

Two Years Old: Hayden wore a yellow raincoat, toddling through the zoo.

Victor released an ecstatic breath and smiled, but when he looked up, the young girl in gray was gone.

Next, a picture of her riding a carnival ride—a big blue turtle—and next to it, a button.

Weeeee! This is fun! Her laugh intoxicating.

Victor turned to the next page. Blank.

The next—blank.

Another page with nothing in it.

"What the hell?" Victor snapped. He turned blank pages until finally a photo.

Seven Years Old: A Halloween Costume—face painted green. A button.

Why can't you go trick-or-treating with me, Daddy?

"I wish I could," Victor whispered.

Then let's go.

"I can't" he cried.

You're always gone.

"Why?" he asked.

Mom says it's because you drink too much. She responded.

Silence followed. He tried pressing it again. *Why can't you go trick or treating with me daddy?*

Victor turned the page. Blank. He turned again until he found more pictures.

Ten Years Old. She's in a gray jersey—kind, warm eyes like her mother's. The girl who was under the table minutes ago smiles in a school photo. Beneath, an obituary.

And a button.

I don't want to go anywhere with you, Dad.

No you're not fine.

Then the sound of a revving engine. Peeling tires. Screaming. A squeal. Crash—metal on metal.

He bursts from under the table. The illusion of his home and wife peeled away to bright white walls. Nurses, patients. Surrounded by figures in blue scrubs, Victor thrashed as they restrained him.

The drunken, faded memory of strapping his eleven-month-old-daughter into the car seat.

A prick in his left arm, and his vision blurred.

"Good morning, Victor," Elena's voice woke him, but it was not her. A nurse stood beside him. "Take these. It'll make you feel better." She set a cup of pills on his bed stand.

He swallowed them and picked up the yellow photo album. "Where's the blue album?"

"You only have *that* one, far as I know," the nurse said as she left the room.

Victor opened the album and flipped through all of Hayden's baby photos, right up until eleven months. Then nothing.

He closed the book and pressed the button on the outside cover—it worked, but the message changed.

I don't want to go anywhere with you, Dad.

He pressed it again, *I don't want to go anywhere with you, Dad.*

With each push of the button, his precious Hayden's voice spoke to him.

I don't want to go anywhere with you, Dad.

Again...

Again...

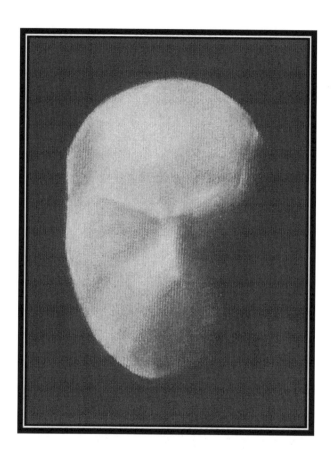

BRUSH WITH FATE

STILL WEARING HER black cocktail dress after the exhibition, Lyssa bound the artist's hands to the bedposts with two silk neckties as instructed. She flipped her hair to one side and tightened the knot around each wrist.

"Tighter," Gavin said.

"This isn't really my thing." She straddled him with a smile. "But I'm game."

She rested back on her haunches over his pelvis. All signs of excitement seemed flaccid. Sweat beads rolled along his hairline.

"Too tight?" she asked.

"Umm..."

"Lyssa," she reminded him. "My name's Lyssa."

"Sorry." He closed his eyes and let out an unsteady sigh. "I need you to do exactly what I say."

Lyssa climbed off him. "Just to be clear, tying you up is fun, but I'm not doing anything weird."

"Take my paint brushes from the dresser there."

"What are we doing with those?" She gave a devilish smirk.

"I know how this is going to sound." Fists clenched, he struggled within the binds. "But all of this sudden interest in my art is a mistake. I need to stop painting. But I can't stop."

Great. The one-night stand was turning into a therapy session. She wasn't a huge fan of his supposed masterpiece series of clown paintings, but perhaps if she jerked off his hubris, he'd be back in the game. "Your work is brilliant."

"It's not my work. Not really. It's those paint brushes." He lowered his voice and spoke through his teeth. "They're evil."

Lyssa slid to the edge of the bed and wished the exit wasn't all the way across the open studio.

"Shut up!" He thrashed from side to side.

"I didn't say anything!"

"Not you."

"Gavin, maybe I should untie you and—"

"No! Take the case of brushes from my dresser. Take it away. The man said those brushes would bring me fame, but at a cost. And I didn't believe it. Of course I didn't believe it." He rapid-fired nonsense faster than Lyssa could keep up. "Take the brushes." Gavin twisted his hands and tugged at the ties, face red and soaked with perspiration. "Destroy them."

"What?" Lyssa scrunched her face at his request.

"I can't explain. Just burn them."

"*You* burn them."

"I can't."

"Why not?"

"I just can't!"

She didn't have to deal with this. Lyssa backed away from the bed and edged toward the exit. "Should I call someone? A friend?" She let out a nervous laugh. "An exorcist?"

"Just take the brushes!"

"No!"

"You're an artist, right? Can't seem to get a leg up in the community? How do you think I became so popular so quickly?" He let out a giggle. "Greatness comes to those who create."

"Are you on something right now?" she asked.

"I *have* to stop." Gavin squeezed his eyes shut and tears spilled down his face. "I'm so tired. I don't care if you use them or burn them, just get them away from me."

Lyssa snatched her heels off the floor.

"Don't you leave here without taking them." Gavin twisted his right hand. The bind loosened around his wrist but not enough to pull free. "Take them or... or I'll fucking kill you!" He kicked his feet to the side, thrusting his weight into the restraint.

Lyssa snagged the leather case from the dresser. A warmth radiated from it as she held it to her chest.

"I can't stop!" Gavin cried.

She clutched the satchel tighter. A sudden need swept over her to keep it for herself. To protect it from Gavin. Cradling the thing with maternal defense, she ran away.

"I can't stop, I can't stop..." he chanted as she flung open the door and ran away.

In the hallway outside Gavin's apartment, she slid on her shoes with trembling hands. Gavin's pounding bed pulsed through the wall, matching the violence of her own heartbeat.

"Wait!" His voice carried through concrete walls.

A neighbor poked his head out of the apartment next door with cat nestled in his arms. "Everything okay?"

Lyssa shook her head. "Asshole threatened to kill me. Call the cops."

The neighbor jumped at the banging from Gavin's apartment. "Yeah, he's been weird lately. Random screaming and such."

"Lyssa!" Gavin hollered through the wall. "Burn them!"

The neighbor nodded, struggling to keep hold of the squirming cat. "Yeah, like *that*."

"What's wrong with him?"

He shrugged. "He's an artist. You know the type."

Lyssa must've pressed the elevator button at least eight times. "Come on," she whispered.

On the ride down to the first floor, she lit a cigarette. She hadn't been this nervous since she placed third in the sixth grade spelling bee. Her father had chastised her about the importance of studying. In the moment when she thought his rage simmered, he grabbed her by the throat. Lyssa's airway was cut off, crushed by her father's hand. It wasn't until her eyes watered and her vision tunneled that he released her. He got in her face, rusty beard scratching her cheek, and snarled through his coffee-stained teeth, "Third place is not good enough!"

In the lobby of Gavin's apartment building, Lyssa's reflection in the glass door seemed to reflect her father's sentiments. *Not good enough.* What the hell was she doing with her life? Art career was a joke. Couldn't manage to sell a painting. Her day job barely covered rent and utilities. She pushed open the door, swiping her reflection aside. Clicking heels ricocheted off towering brick walls, and with each step, the case of brushes vexed her. Maybe she shouldn't have taken them.

Conflicting thoughts waned with each step she took away from Gavin. Nicotine helped calm her nerves as she slid her key into the rusted car door.

A man's muffled scream came from above. Gavin stood at the fifth floor window, banging on the glass. "Lyssa!" His voice grew louder as he pushed the paned window fully open. "Wait!"

From across the street, Lyssa paused for whatever new absurdity Gavin would spew. He leaned on the windowsill in silence, like he was trying to figure out how to apologize.

"What do you want?" she shouted.

"I changed my mind. I want them back!"

No. They belonged to her now.

He planted a knee in the windowsill.

"What are you doing?" *Crazy son of a bitch.*

Gavin heaved himself into the opening.

Lyssa's blood drained to her feet, anchoring her to the pavement.

Gavin stretched both arms toward her. Before she could react, he dove headfirst.

Lyssa's scream became trapped behind a shrill gasp. All the things she could have done, all the ways she could have helped him, ran through her head. In that instant of eternity, she froze while Gavin Francisco plummeted to the pavement with a bone-shattering thud.

Deep crimson splattered across the sidewalk like a Jackson Pollock. Gavin's body lay broken beside a parking meter, and Lyssa's shriek finally cut free, echoing through the neighborhood.

Two weeks later, the leather case remained unopened, sitting on her coffee table. An intense curiosity attracted her each time she walked by, but after what happened to Gavin, she'd been reluctant to address it. From within their confines, the brushes begged her to open them. To let them breathe life into a painting. Two weeks, tossing and turning, haunted more by their incessant call than by the memory of Gavin's tragic death.

Jax, her connection at the gallery, reclined on her couch stroking his well-oiled beard. "The Met wants his work."

"Are you serious?" Lyssa asked.

"Yep. Morris told me today. They're buying Gavin Francisco's work. Calling him the artist of the decade, maybe even the century."

"For the clown paintings?"

"Yeah."

Lyssa sank into the couch with her glass of wine, eyeing the leather case. Perhaps if she opened it, she would have the same kind of luck as Gavin. Or maybe the same fate. The uncertainty kept her from opening the damn thing for the past two weeks.

"Is that the set you told me about?" Jax asked.

Lyssa had left out the part about the supposed curse. She nodded.

"Are you going to open them?" Jax reached for the case.

"No," Lyssa blurted, blocking his hand.

He leaned back and looked to her with a head tilt. "He asked you to take the brushes. You don't have to feel shame in having them."

"That's not it."

"Maybe he saw something in you." Jax scooted closer on the couch. "You're incredibly talented. Maybe he wanted you to carry on his work after his death." Jax placed his hand on her knee.

Smooth. Lyssa pulled away and reached for her glass of wine. "Don't start with that, Jax."

"With what?"

"You know. You find female artists, pump up our self-esteem, make us think we have a shot at an exhibition, and then you get us to sleep with you—"

"That's not how it is."

187

Lyssa raised an eyebrow. "I'm not naïve. I knew what I was doing when I slept with you. I knew you might never recommend me to Morris and the board."

"Are you saying you slept with me in hopes that you'd get an exhibition?"

"It's not like it worked," Lyssa laughed. She feigned a serious face and rested her jaw on her fist. "So when other women sleep with you, does *their* work get put to the top of the recommendation list? How does that work?"

"I can't believe you right now." Jax stood, clenching his fists.

"Oh please. Can you blame me? Do you know how hard it is to get recognized in this community if you don't have a penis?"

Jax bit his lip as if holding back profanities and backed toward the door. "Is that why you were at Francisco's that night? Hoping you could ride his cock to fame?"

"Fuck you, Jax!"

"You already did!" He blazed out of her apartment.

After Jax had left, Lyssa tossed back the rest of her wine.

Resting her elbows on her knees, she drew the weathered satchel closer. It begged to be opened, but a warning deep inside, as strong as her curiosity to open it, implored her to keep away.

Now that she had pissed off Jax, her gallery connection was shattered. These brushes might hold the secret to her fame. They could be her only chance. Lyssa shook her head at the ridiculous thought, reminding herself that she was not the superstitious type.

"Screw it." She unwound the leather strap from the tattered satchel. What looked like burn marks scorched the edge. As she bent back the flap, the aroma of old leather and oil paint spilled from the case and saturated her soul.

Ten black-handled brushes were tucked into individual pockets.

Attracted to the oak handles, her fingers ran along their rough edges. Bits of remnant paint crusted to the ferrules told stories of their past. Stories of great artists and sleepless nights at the easel. Tears, anger, blissfulness. Some ancient energy pulsed within them, beating in sync with her heart.

She pulled back from the spell the old tools had cast on her and crossed her arms. It was too late to paint anyway. Wavering from either the wine or exhaustion, Lyssa's head nodded off.

A chill wrapped around her spine and drew her back to the brushes.

Stitched on the inside flap of the case was a frayed piece of fabric. Embroidered in black Old English lettering:

Greatness comes to those who create.

Death to those who stop.

She heard the words in her father's voice. He had always pushed her to achieve greatness, but no matter how hard she tried, she failed him. She was not good enough. She'd never be good enough, and his devotion to making sure she knew that never ceased until his death.

Her thundering heart pleaded to set the brushes loose onto a canvas. They needed to create—to bring life to the plain white emptiness—and they commissioned Lyssa to do the job. One round-tip brush between her fingers, she held it up for closer inspection. It made a silent promise to forge her legacy.

Lyssa whispered under her breath, "Greatness comes to those who create."

Black and white dollops of oil squeezed out of tubes and onto the palette. The handle of the large brush generated a soft static, an energy, seeping into her skin and filtering through her blood. That static filled the apartment and charged her with inspiration. An uncontrollable drive to create.

A glob of white with a swirl of black touched the canvas and sparked a storm. It wisped into overcast—heavy and foreboding like the clouds on the coast after the spelling bee.

Fresh bruises on her neck, Lyssa had snuck outside to the dunes. Incoming storm clouds devoured an orange sunset as another girl about her age ran along the shoreline. The child in a cadmium red raincoat danced in the wind as waves crashed against her ankles. A shameless, awkward ballet of an amateur. Defiant of the storm, the girl laughed and twirled along the beach without a care. Hidden in the tall grass on the dunes, Lyssa wished she could be like that girl. Without fear of the incoming storm. Without fear of incompetence or failure. *Good enough* as is.

Lyssa's knees buckled, snapping her from the trance. Having nearly fallen asleep at the canvas, she took a step back. Three hours had passed already.

The looming storm off the coast stood as the backdrop to an unfinished figure in the foreground.

Where'd she come from?

Lyssa didn't recall painting beyond the black and white clouds, but there it was. A perfectly executed landscape, along with what would eventually be the portrait of the little girl in the raincoat. Thick cadmium base strokes laid the foundation of her body. Smears of beige and tan marked her face, underdeveloped like a fetus, featureless. Even without eyes, she somehow stared out of the canvas, imploring to be finished, to be *more*.

Eyes dry, legs tired, Lyssa needed to sleep. Maybe if Jax hadn't slept over the night before, she wouldn't be so exhausted. Despite her desire to finish, she staggered into her bedroom—a shoebox of a space with a curtained-off closet at the foot of the bed. Changing out of her paint-splattered jeans would require too much effort, so she left them on and collapsed face-first onto the sheets. Imprinted on the back of her lids was the unfinished figure of the girl on the beach.

Lyssa sprang upright in the darkness, waking from a horrible dream she couldn't remember. Scant city light slipped through broken blinds.

From the closet, a small voice hissed, "Death to those who stop."

Lyssa froze. The dark void beyond the curtain's part attracted her eyes with the force of a black hole. As she was

191

about to disregard the voice as part of a waking nightmare, the outline of a small person appeared in the closet.

Lyssa slid her legs to the edge of the bed. Sanity tried to reclaim its place in her mind, dismissing the form as nothing more than her imagination giving shape to hanging clothes. But that voice replayed in her head.

The curtain fluttered, but the air current in the room wasn't strong enough to move it. She focused her eyes in the darkness, trying to make sense of it.

Lyssa lowered her feet to the floor, then edged closer to the light switch by the closet.

What looked like a face could easily be the sleeve of a shirt. Lyssa's vision honed in. There were no discernible eyes or any other facial features. She sighed with relief until she recalled the faceless fetus—the painting of the girl in the red raincoat.

As she closed in, the illusion of the girl did not falter.

She turned to hit the switch and the light blared on.

Betrayed by her tired eyes, Lyssa pulled open the curtains and released her breath upon finding nothing. Shaken, she left the light on and crawled back into bed. When she closed her eyes and rolled onto her side, she heard it again.

"Death to those who stop."

Moist breath clung to Lyssa's face. She opened her eyes to the faceless painted girl crouched bedside, inches away. The aroma of linseed oil and turpentine strong enough to taste on her tongue.

Slimy hands thrust out and clutched Lyssa's trachea so tight she couldn't scream. Lyssa grabbed at the arms, slippery with paint, and tried to pry the girl from her neck.

Despite her lack of eyes, brush strokes along the painted girl's brow carved a dire expression. A black mouth split open and growled, "Death to those who stop."

The quaking voice rattled Lyssa from the inside. Her teeth chattered. Vibrations skittered through her blood.

She fought away from the girl's grasp, but couldn't break from the tremors crawling inside her bones. Feet tangling in the top sheet, she scrambled across her bed and spilled to the floor. While running from the room, Lyssa looked back, but the girl was no longer there.

It's just sleep deprivation.

Lack of sleep could have been causing hallucinations, but the fresh smears of paint on her hands and neck proved the reality. Lyssa wiped the paint from her palms onto her pants and paced the apartment, trying to avoid the painting.

Death to those who stop.

"I didn't stop." Lyssa laughed and murmured under her breath. "I'm talking to a fucking painting." She shook her head. "I'll finish tomorrow."

"Now," it whispered in her head. Lyssa screeched, covering her ears, but the audible hallucination was unavoidable.

"Shut up!" Lyssa ran to open a window. The creepy thing, real or not, would haunt her all night if she didn't get rid of it. She grabbed the four-by-six painting by the frame and flung it out the window. It crashed into the alley, missing the dumpster below. If her father were still alive, he'd reprimand her for quitting, but she didn't have to answer to him anymore.

The brushes summoned her.

With shaking hands, she gathered them. She had to get rid of the damn things. Even if they weren't cursed, they were causing a psychological breakdown. Lyssa learned long ago, it wasn't that hard to put an end to tormenting things. Her father's truculent behavior exploded into nothingness with no more than a flick of the gas stove's knob.

Somehow, the remnant ash of his presence still found its way into her lungs, suffocating her every chance it got.

She shook him from her memory.

A stainless steel pot on the stove would make the perfect burn bin. She'd set the brushes on fire. Like Gavin had directed.

As she held a lighter and some torn shreds of paper kindling, Lyssa couldn't move forward. Something inside, something instinctual, prohibited her.

The brushes *needed* her. And she needed them.

Lyssa pushed against their will and lit a shred of paper. Sweat trickled down her hairline. Her heart raced, full body tremors. Flames ate away at the paper, encroaching upon her fingers.

Just drop it in the pot.

Something else took control. A force outside of herself— magnetic in nature, powerful. Each time she drew close, she was pushed back and the flames sputtered out.

No matter how many times she lit the paper and tried, she couldn't.

Once she finally gave up, the brushes allowed her to come close again, as if they *knew* her intentions. She placed each brush into the case, put up surrendering hands, and backed away. Unsure what to do, Lyssa retreated to the couch and lay down. Clutching a pillow to her chest, she hoped to wake up free from whatever was happening to her.

As she began to doze off, her breath was stolen away. A canvas of black fabric smothered her. With the pillow pressed firm to her face, she struggled beneath, kicking, swatting. She rolled to her side and gasped for a breath, then thrust the pillow away. Smeared on the fabric, was fresh oil paint. Crimson and beige.

"What do you want?" She rocked herself on the couch, pulling in fast short breaths, and scratching at her ears.

The voice tremored within. *Death to those who stop.*

Lyssa's upper lip curled. "Not if I stop you first." She charged toward the kitchen for her lighter and the jar of turpentine. Maybe she couldn't destroy the brushes, but she could do something about *her*.

Turpentine splashing over the rim of the jar, she rushed down her apartment stairwell. Outside, in the alley, she approached the fallen painting. The top right corner of the frame had cracked. With the canvas leaning against a dumpster, Lyssa poured turpentine over the girl. An inchoate face streaked with white and gray as chemicals pulled the colors of the clouds through her. Lyssa held the lighter to the edge.

195

Flames devoured the little girl.

The oils of her face blistered and popped. Burnt chemicals turned to tendrils of smoke. Lyssa choked on the fumes.

Without even a breeze, the fire was extinguished in an instant.

"No." She tried to light it again, but it wouldn't catch.

Again. Not even a spark from her lighter.

She knelt by the painting and broke down. Tears spilled down her cheeks.

Only losers cry, Dad would have said. She wiped away her tears.

"I don't know what to do."

Greatness comes to those who create. It reverberated through her core.

Lyssa climbed her apartment stairs, dragging the painting behind her.

She chucked it inside her apartment, closed the door, and sat out in the hallway. Defeated, she slunk down to the floor with her back against the door.

Tears escaped her again, but she caught her hitching breath to regain control. When she looked up, the painted girl was back. Her crude form now blistered and melted, as Lyssa had left her on the canvas. Black char crusted on craters of mutated paint.

The surreal girl rushed at her in awkward, jerking movements. She threw herself at Lyssa as her raincoat ignited into an inferno.

Scalded by the fire, Lyssa shrieked. Agonizing, guttural howls of despair as her flesh peeled from her face. Through the pain, she struggled to get to her feet.

Jax charged up the stairs and the fire dissipated as quickly as it formed. "Lyssa!" He hurried to her side.

Caterwauling and drooling, she inspected for burns or blisters. "Help me!"

"What's wrong?"

"Am I okay? Is it bad?"

"Is what bad?" Jax asked.

"The burns." Lyssa's fingers explored her skin, but nothing felt out of the ordinary. "The fire..."

"What fire? Lyssa, there's no fire."

"Just now..." Even to her own ears, she sounded crazy. It would never end and she'd never rest. If she stopped, she'd die. But if she finished her creation... *greatness.* "Actually. I think I was having a nightmare or something."

"Like sleepwalking?"

"Yeah. Crazy right?" A breathy chuckle dribbled out of her—a hysterical sound, laced with her looming sanity.

Jax helped her to her feet and offered to sit with her inside her apartment, but Lyssa shoved him away. "No. I can't stop. I can't stop."

She locked herself inside, set the canvas on her easel and scraped off the damage from the fire.

Head lolling from exhaustion, she went back to work.

There was no way out of this without finishing.

With careful hands she fabricated the raincoat with shades of cadmium and crimson. It billowed in the summer storm as the little girl danced. A fine brush honed in on the face. She tried to remember that child from her past—how carefree and happy she was. Free from the embarrassment of inadequacy. Free from the drive to succeed. The little girl in red was perfectly content. Perfectly good enough.

Something jarred Lyssa from her trance.

She stepped back to examine the painting and the dancing girl seemed to smile back, content with Lyssa's work.

A knock drew her attention to the daylight coming in the window.

She opened the door to Jax.

"I'm just checking in after last night. You alright?" he asked.

Lyssa twitched, unsure of her state.

"Jesus, look at your ears. Is that blood?"

Her fingers traversed bits of crusted blood where she had been scratching to silence the painted girl.

He looked past her toward the painting. "You've been painting. Is that paint on your ears?"

"Yeah," she agreed.

"Couldn't sleep last night?" Jax let himself in.

Waiting for the painted girl to show up, Lyssa's eyes pinballed the room.

"You're acting weird," Jax said.

"You know us artist types." She crossed her arms and laughed at herself.

"This is..." Jax leaned in closer to the girl on the beach. "Brilliant."

"Brilliant like Gavin Francisco?"

He held his hand to his heart. "Maybe even better. It's like it's *alive*."

"You have no idea," she said.

"I need to show Morris." He held up his phone to take a picture.

After Jax had left, she sank into the couch, relieved to be done, but anxious that the painted girl would return.

She jumped up from the couch in a sudden panic.

Was it back?

The clock read three o'clock in the afternoon. She had slept for six hours. Finally, it left her alone.

Jax knocked then rushed in without waiting for her to answer. He rambled on about how he went to see the curator, Mr. Morris, and that he liked what he saw in the photo.

"An *exhibition*," Jax said.

"For the beach painting? That was fast. He hasn't even seen it in person yet."

"You should've seen the look on his face. He was smitten."

"By her?" Lyssa stared into the girl's eyes, keeping their secret.

"By you. By everything. I don't know if Francisco's death inspired you or what, but this..." He gestured to the painting. "This is spectacular."

She could feel a sinuous smile slithering between her lips.

Greatness comes to those who create.

"Lyssa! Hello?" Jax waved his hand in front of her face. "A gallery show. For you. But..."

Lyssa perked up. "But what?"

"Morris wants more. A series of paintings tied to this one."

"He wants me to paint more?" Her heart shuddered at the thought of using the brushes ever again.

"Give him a series and you're in, babe."

Jax came and left in a storm of excitement with promises of her own gallery show.

More paintings.

The set of brushes were strewn about her workspace. Some soaked in turpentine, others lay upon her palette, scattered about like casualties of war. She picked up each one, and carefully cleaned the bits of paint from their bristles and set them upright in a mug.

How many sleepless nights of painting could she suffer through, haunted by her own creations, to get the recognition she so badly wanted? So badly *deserved*.

Just a few more paintings and she could pawn the brushes off on someone else. Maybe Jax. Just a few more and the Met would be begging for *her* work.

A series.

The night after the spelling bee, after the little girl in red had vanished down the shoreline, a fishing boat appeared on the horizon. Lyssa thought about that boat from time to time, and how the fisherman must've handled that storm. She pictured a man in a tattered coat, grayed, too worn and weathered to know its original color. Black rubber galoshes protected his feet from the surge spilling over the hull. Chains and hooks slung over his shoulder like something out of an old horror story. That's how she imagined fishermen back then. Large and foreboding, laughing at the storm's feeble attempt. "Is that all you've got!" the man would scream. "It's not good enough!"

Lyssa released a breath as if she'd been holding it for days. As soon as the inspiration struck, the brushes called for her to paint again. Their pulse undulated as she prepared another canvas.

Hands shaking, she squeezed some cobalt and black onto her palette. Dark static filled the air while great waves crashed in the night. A frenzy of grays and blues washed over her mind for hours. She fought through exhaustion, pumping herself full of caffeine until her eyes grew heavy and her body defied her will to continue.

Lyssa lifted her head from the countertop. She must've fallen asleep right after pouring her coffee.

Behind her, hefty sloshing footsteps approached.

Death to those who stop. The familiar nemesis returned, quaking within her core.

An intrusive stench of turpentine and linseed oil wafted in with it. She turned slowly to confront whatever she had created.

Well over six feet tall, he loomed, carrying a massive hook swaying from a black stroke of paint—what would later be a chain. Slick and dripping with fresh oils, the fisherman's face came into the light of the overhead lamp. Strong cheekbones. Dark familiar eyes.

"No. Not you." Lyssa staggered back, chin quivering. She pleaded, "I'll finish. I promise."

Bearing his coffee-stained teeth from behind a rusty gnarled beard, her painted father grabbed her by the throat and pinned her to the wall. "That's not good enough!"

EMPTY NEST

HANDS LOCKED ON THE kitchen counter, Joe stares at the oven clock. The glowing green digital numbers read 11:59. Pulse murky, gut twisting, he hopes it will never change. That it'll stay 11:59 forever. He would stand like this, petrified in time, as punishment.

12:00.

The anniversary gut-punches him. He's been anticipating the blow, but it knocks the wind out of him anyway. A vice squeezes his heart, his lungs, his trachea. He can't breathe. Crippling pain chokes him into the fetal position.

An entire year has passed since he lost them. Joe's not sure if he'll survive another. Too much for a man to bear. Every night, they visit his dreams, begging Joe to pick them up. If only they called him that dreaded night last year. He never should have let them go.

"Joe," Jessica runs to his side and hovers over him. "Breathe."

But the excruciating vice of loss forbids it. Tears drain in a deluge. His mouth hangs open, trying to scream, but that torturous grip on his lungs strangles him into silence.

"Breathe, Joe."

A harsh grunt escapes. Then a gasp of undeserving air stabs his lungs. Another, another.

"You're hyperventilating. Slow breaths," Jessica says.

Sobs pulse from his core like blood from a severed artery. He wishes he were bleeding out instead. Bleeding until everything goes black so he wouldn't feel the treacherous torment of their absence. Saliva and mucous string from his face while Jessica holds him in her arms.

Last night, Lily came to him with flames in her tearful eyes. There were no smiles on his children's faces in his dream—his nightmare. An inferno raged behind them. Ben's tiny hands extended for help, but Joe couldn't reach him. Lily begged for him to come get them. He wishes it were that simple—to drive over and take them away from that house. Lily's fire-wreathed eyes burned her cheeks when she cried. She implored that Joe come for them right away.

Lily usually had a way of lighting up his heart. Wherever there was Lily, there was light. But Joe's life has been nothing but dark and frigid for the past year.

Joe sits in the passenger seat with a bouquet of roses laid across his lap while Jessica drives him to the house.

"Do you want me to come with you?" Jessica pulls up to the property.

"No. I need to do this alone." He steps out of the car, bouquet dangling upside down from his weak fingers.

Overcast skies press down, crushing Joe so hard he's not sure he can make the walk up the path. The landscape darkens around the burnt remains of the structure—what used to be called *home*. It sits about fifty yards back from the road. Blackened beams and warped siding tell its violent story.

He used to live there with them, back when he and Elaine were young and had an entire lifetime ahead of them. Back when the kids were babies and Elaine was clean. He should've fought harder in court for full custody. He should've offered to take the kids on Elaine's weekend instead of going on a date with Jessica. Elaine forgot it was her weekend anyway, so he could've gotten away with it. The kids would still be around to light up his day and warm his heart... if only he tried harder.

The crusted charred remains of their home loom over him. The porch's rotting burnt floorboards groan under his weight. Joe hangs his head. Grief squeezes all that's worth living for out of his lungs. Teardrops splash to the porch's wooden slats.

Joe collapses to his knees, hunched and writhing in waves of despair. He wishes he could crawl inside and burn to death with them.

A light shines in from the east. A part in the clouds on the horizon. The column of orange sunlight dances across the petals of the roses. Joe sets them down. He's unsure why he bothered bringing them. In a few days, the petals will turn as black and lifeless as this house.

He stands and wipes away tears that won't stop falling.

An orange light flickers in the gaps between the warped shiplap. Joe shakes his head of the illusion and peers into the black space. A misplaced sunbeam falls upon blackened walls. Walls that should have held the memories of their childhood. The place they should have called *home.*

Instead, it became a house of sadness and overdose. A house of bad relationships and nightmares. A blackened burnt-out shell of a place that could never be anything other than a home to death.

This was no place for his children, it never was.

Joe stares at the odd orange light that doesn't belong and holds out his hands. Radiating heat on his palms. He closes his eyes, shuddering as the hands of his children slide into his. If he opens his eyes, he fears they'll be gone.

With the thermal touch of the sun on his hands, a touch he hasn't felt in too long, Joe keeps his eyes shut and guides the kids away from the house of death. Lily's light and Ben's warmth follow him. Daylight shines through the clouds and fills the backseat of the car as Joe gets in and brings his children home.

About the Author

RED LAGOE grew up on 80s horror and carried her paranoia of slashers and sewer creatures into adulthood. Horror stories have always been in her head, but instead of using her ever-so-useful Independent Studies degree in a creative field, she went to work in the veterinary field. Here, she learned first-hand to identify the smell of death and burnt flesh. She's had her hands inside the warm abdominal cavities of living things, and assisted on surgeries where limbs and eyeballs were removed. Putrid infections, maggots, rabies, and diseases riddled her day to day. She put seven years of her own (literal) blood, sweat, and tears into her job but needed to step away.

Red made the painful decision to leave her beloved nine-to-five to spend more time with her kids and to pursue her buried passion for writing dark fiction.

When she's not spewing her horror-ridden mind onto the page, or substituting at the elementary school like a normal upstanding citizen, Red enjoys amateur astronomy, and can be found lingering in the inky shadows among beasts for a better view of the stars.

Red's Stories and Where to Find Them

Consumer Alert placed sixth in the Dark Regions Press contest and will appear in the 2020 release, *Black Labyrinth: Possessions*.

Never Have I Ever: Sinister Smile Press', *If I Die Before I Wake, Vol. 2*

Prospect Nowhere: Dark Moon Digest, *issue 38*

Flicker: Sinister Smile Press, *If I Die Before I Wake, Vol. 1*

Memory Lane, Long Distance Cull (co-written with Tony Logan), **Malignant Roots,** & **Odor Mortis:** all published by Crystal Lake Publishing, *Shallow Waters Volumes 1–4*.

Best Seat in the House: Horror Tree, *Trembling with Fear Year Two*

Luna's Lure: Owl Hollow Press, *Under the Full Moon's Light*

Missing Souls: Z Publishing's *America's Emerging Horror Writers, East Region*

The Haunting Murder: Z Publishing's *Virginia's Emerging Writers*

Helping Hands Retreat: Toasted Cheese Literary Journal's 2016 Dead of Winter Horror Contest, 3rd place.

Fair Haven: Red's viral apocalypse debut novel 2017

CONTENT WARNING

Loss of children and parental grief
are depicted in these stories:

Lucid Screaming:
Loss of children portrayed. Brief depiction of a child's
body. Mother hears children screaming.

Memory Lane:
Loss of child implied.
Father suffers with grief.

Empty Nest:
Loss of children discussed, but not depicted.
Father suffers with grief and guilt.

Made in the USA
Columbia, SC
19 July 2021

42103465R00115